Crossings 31

The passage from *The Emigrants* by W.G. Sebald is from the Michael Hulse translation for New Directions.

Library of Congress Cataloging-in-Publication Data

Names: Magliani, Marino, 1960- author. | Scalzo, Zachary, translator.
Title: A window to Zeewijk / Marino Magliani, Zachary Scalzo.
Other titles: Soggiorno a Zeewijk. English
Description: New York : Bordighera Press, [2021] | Series: Crossings; 31 | An English translation from the Italian. | Summary: "Set between the Netherlands and the end of western Liguria, Marino Magliani traces a geography of the humane and the forlorn, of panoramas and yearning. "A Window to Zeewijk" is the story of a changing landscapes, of houses with lifespans shorter than that their inhabitants. A chance encounter leads readers down trails of joy and melancholy, as everything seems to be in Zeewijk"-- Provided by publisher.
Identifiers: LCCN 2021028085 | ISBN 9781599541785 (paperback)
Subjects: LCGFT: Novels.
Classification: LCC PQ4913.A36 S6413 2021 | DDC 853/.92--dc23
LC record available at https://lccn.loc.gov/2021028085

Printed in the United States.

Published by
BORDIGHERA PRESS
John D. Calandra Italian American Institute
25 W. 43rd Street, 17th Floor
New York, NY 10036

Crossings 31
ISBN 978-1-59954-178-5

A Window to Zeewijk

A Window to Zeewijk

Marino Magliani

Translated by Zachary Scalzo

BORDIGHERA PRESS

Dimore segrete
  dove si nomina il giorno per signoria monotona di lampi.

FRANCESCO MAROTTA, *PER SOGLIE D'INCREATO*

Forse il segreto è essere quello che si è, scoprirsi felici senza nessun motivo, per qualcosa che è accaduto prima e continuerà ad accadere.

FABRIZIO CENTOFANTI, *STELLE*

No todos estuvieron de acuerdo en que ésa fuera, en efecto, la cuestión.

PABLO D'ORS, *LECCIONES DE ILUSIÓN*

PREFACE

Italian writers (or maybe just writers in general) are blurring into each other nowadays. They are the product of Creative Writing classes, of Academic seminars, and of sanitized corporate-speak. Their sentences are short and their language elementary, accessible to all, often trivial, imitating advertisements and the way they speak. Their stories chase crime news, looking for morbid details, family tragedies, political messages. But Literature has always been something else. Its characters are full of life, its sentences are charged with energy, even commas have a personality. And a great novel or a great poem is not similar to anything else, and it is not replicating anyone else: it is completely distinct. And this is what makes them works of art. Artists do not care what their audiences need, what is commercially useful or correct; they look for beauty, and they look for it everywhere, even in ugliness.

Marino Magliani is an original, wild writer. When Magliani writes — he actually paints, sculpts, films. All your senses are stimulated. You will read this novel, in the magnificent translation of Zachary Scalzo, and you won't find one weak, anonymous line; each sentence is a vision, crafted with passion. The architecture of his stories and of his syntax is not similar to anything else in contemporary Italian Literature. Maybe you can find some traces in the history of literature: in Kafka and the great South American novelists and poets or in Italo Calvino and Francesco Biamonti. And speaking of Calvino and Biamonti, Marino Magliani is from Liguria, too, a son of that narrow, harsh region, tightly gripped between the aggressive sea to the South and the jagged mountains to the North. Magliani's prose — in this novel as elsewhere — absorbs those colors, nuances, fragrances and, in *A Window to Zeewijk*, overlaps them continuously with the colors of a little Dutch suburb not far from Amsterdam, where Magliani currently lives.

As a matter of fact, while inspired by his native land, Magliani is a citizen of the world. Having left when he was young, looking for jobs and adventure, he lived in Costa Brava, where he translated the menus of all the Italian restaurants, and on the Canary Islands. When he left Spain, he moved to South America, in the Pampas, where among other jobs, he worked as a ship boy, a docker, a manual laborer, a day laborer, and a translator.

Magliani's first book, *Molo Express*, appeared in 1999. But critics began to take note of him with the publication of *Quattro giorni per non morire* (Sironi, 2006), and today he is among the most respected Italian writers whose works have been translated in Germany, France, Spain, Holland, Romania, Poland, Argentina, Chile, and other countries. In addition to his novels, he has translated a number of books from Spanish, including works by Roberto Arlt, Fernando Velázquez Medina, Haroldo Conti, Pablo d'Ors, and Adrián Giménez.

Originally published by Amos edizioni from Mestre, Venice, I feel proud to present to American readers Marino Magliani and *A Window to Zeewijk*.

Emanuele Pettener
JUNE 2021

OVERLAPPING BLUES AND GRAYS

Imagine you own a house, one you can reach only by using a path through sandy barriers and lakeside vistas about which all you'd think to say if anyone were to ask is that they really slowed you down when you were trying to go home. But you can't imagine this, because this path and the house's front door are one and the same: they're exactly what they are, that's how it is, and you can't compare them to anything else. Imagine, then, that around one hundred fifty years ago someone created a second door, a magical gate of a canal dug to connect the North Sea to a port and a bay that, until then, could only be reached by a long trip through the Zuiderzee.

That is the true story of the birth of Zeewijk. The neighborhood in this book.

The 'house' reached only by traversing sands and marshes is called Amsterdam, but you can forget that fact. The new beginning is the Noordzee-kanaal—twenty or so kilometers long and a few hundred meters wide and containing three locks—but these details, too, are unimportant.

Zeewijk is a neighborhood on the sea. And that's the point. "Zee" is "the sea," "wijk" "the neighborhood."

Between Zeewijk and the canal to its north stands the Port of IJmuiden. To the south and the west there are dunes and woodlands, and the city of IJmuiden—where Zeewijk is found—extends to the east. It belongs to the Velsen municipality in the province of Noord Holland (what they call a province, we might call a region.)

The IJmuiden neighborhood next to Zeewijk is called Duinwijk, but that's not really true since Duinwijk doesn't really exist. It's a made-up name for a part of Zeewijk where few foreigners reside, made up so they—that is, the citizens of Duinwijk—could say that they do not live in Zeewijk.

When you see it on a map, Zeewijk looks like two other lands. One is the south of Norway, that bit out near Trondheim, except the only difference is that Norway lies vertically while Zeewijk lies along the North Sea.

The other land that Zeewijk disquietingly reminds you of is the province of Imperia, that appendage on the bowed-over seaside body they call Liguria.

It's true. If you play with the scale a bit and try to put Zeewijk on top of Imperia, you'll find they are the same exact shape. The same curves, the same corners. And if you do the same with its neighbor, IJmuiden, tracing the asphalt lanes of Heerenduinweg (the dunes are to the south) and the bricked ones of Kromhoutstraat (which becomes Kanaaldijk, the main road above the dike), you'll find . . . It's incredible, isn't it? IJmuiden without Zeewijk takes the same shape as Liguria without Imperia, a half-sad mouth, and it's as if its natural extension, IJmuiden, is there, too—in Savona, Genoa, La Spezia.

One thinks he reached this land by chance so many years ago, and the sad coincidence of these maps denies it.

I

Zeewijk was founded on sand. Before it was a neighborhood, it was the wind from the sea. Twisted oaks and torn grasses.

But all of that changed after the canal. That was how Piet Van Bert explained it to me.

Sand is a kind of clastic rock, one that you get from the constant erosion of sandstone. This means 90% of Liguria sits on sandstone. But sand can also be formed from bone debris, shells and skeletons, from the sea, as is the case for Zeewijk.

From even my earliest glimpses of Zeewijk, and maybe even before I had met Piet, I had already realized that certain pathways—the ones between the dunes and the hollows recently covered by vegetation—presented a sizeable stratum of shell dust. According to Piet, the contact between sedimentary sandstone and stone which formed by other means—from ionically charged rains, for example, or, in our case, from a concentration of skeletal dust—creates a number of disturbing phenomena. One of these is a *filled time*.

It's as if time in Zeewijk depends on the cross-contamination of the particles in its sandy foundation.

In fact, the dune itself provides us with the perfect demonstration of Piet Van Bert's theory: no single part of a dune keeps its shape as is for long, but it still retains a primal essence. "For long" is meant not in archeological terms, but in purely human ones. A season, a cycle of seasons. We know that a dune begins to form as a grain of sand comes to rest on an object—a blade of grass, for example, collects one grain and so on until, in time, that same accumulation takes away its own height and form. The dune disappears, it moves. Until one day—and this is true, and even if it takes a long time, it does happen—it reforms itself, it remakes itself again as it was in the past.

So, as if following this star, Zeewijk—Piet insists—was built, respecting the exact environment that created it and each characteristic that regulates it.

The sand on which the neighborhood sits is a mixture of original sand and that which was excavated after 1860, beached in the canal's creation. It's a monument that brings all sands together. Not taking into account the reality of each moment in the neighborhood's creation would have meant upsetting the sense of things.

"Zeewijk was my father's dream. Willem Leonard Van Bert. IJmuiden's expansion—the expansion of Holland—that's what Zeewijk is . . ."

We were at his house. He was standing in front of the window, his back to me as he looked out on his back garden, which consisted of a raised row of *Calluna vulgaris* invaded by *Ribes giraldii*—a plant I've to this day only seen in his garden despite how long I've lived in Zeewijk and a plant he'd cultivated to attract the only blue rock thrushes in all of Northern Europe, greedy for the currants that hung from them.

"IJmuiden was supposed to expand towards the sea. To the west, like every migration. My father was a city councilor and he cared about those things."

I recreate our full conversation here, something I can do faithfully because back then I would—and have recently begun to do again—write down our discussions.

I asked Piet what he meant by "building and taking the sand into account."

I'll admit that I hadn't learned a single word of Dutch (I'd arrived in Holland a year earlier in the winter of 1989 and had worked as a dockworker in the port) and I would speak to Piet in English or French.

Piet didn't understand. "I meant what I meant," he said.

"Right. But was there a particular architectural design that considered the sand? I don't know. Were there long, low buildings that look like the mice and moles you'd find on the dunes, and they would create some kind of harmony with the land? Why don't we prefer houses with windmills next to them, like I've seen in other Northern coasts—like in Wijk aan Zee?"

No, he said. Nothing was to be invented in Zeewijk. After all, granulometry in art was nothing new—just think of Flaubert's obsession with sand.

Zeewijk's taste for buildings, for lines of buildings welded to each other and for *maisonettes* and its schools and malls did not differ at all from classic "Dutch" architecture, were it not for their unbroken rows.

The harmony—and maybe this was what was new—had to depend on time. He said that in Zeewijk a building, be it a house or a school or even a hospital, had a very short lifespan. Forty years at most, and then it was replaced with another. This is how it respected its environment.

It followed the schedule of the nature of sand: a dune exhausted itself and, in its place, destiny (or, the wind) built another, but different—narrower or longer, lower or more bare, covered in locks of northern *sambucus*, the poisonous kind so that it might not be martyred by the assaults of birds.

Zeewijk was a training. An installation. A repetition. As was typical, he would turn his back to me and speak to the window, frosted with a crust of salt as if it had been spat upon.

Outside, the wind moved the *ribes* frond, which slapped at the air as if lifting a skirt. In the long silences that followed our complaints and debates, it was almost as if we weren't there—which is to say that we remained there unthinking, unremembering, and unrushed, standing with our hands on our hips like photographers with our cameras on our shoulders, waiting for the right conditions to take the exact same photograph again and again, through the same window with the same light and at the same angle.

Piet would call it an exercise of resistance. After a while, I'd laugh.

One day Piet brought me to the roof of a building that, obviously, no longer exists and he pointed out things on the horizon. They were romantic things, ones that no young man could remember ever having existed. He had foreseen all of that, but not the change in their use. As far as that was concerned, the Van Berts had no power anymore as they, too, had disappeared, transformed, now a decayed dynasty of engineers and councilors reached its lowest rank with its final inheritor: Piet Van Bert, a man who had interrupted his study of architecture, a man now jobless and collecting unemployment, his only possible occupation being a flâneur of the sands. What he had not foreseen, however, was that it was not that building's future from which we had looked to the horizon—to know that, you'd have to be on a list somewhere or on IJmuiden's planning committee or on the committees of various Co-ops that divide and manage housing in IJmuiden and, truly, all of Holland.

Now, it's clear that Piet was right: Nothing in Zeewijk has lasted, or lasts, like it does anywhere else.

From 1988 to today, they have demolished a shopping center from the seventies, one that was still in excellent condition, and, in its place, they raised another on the exact same sandy foundation. It's called Zeewijkpassage and it even attracts the exact same clientele. Since 1988, they have destroyed a hospital built in the seventies and soon they will erect a large swath of condominiums on its sand. Since 1988, they've demolished at least three schools built after the war (here, anything that isn't sand is dated *after the war*, a perfect formula to archaeologically describe Zeewijk's urban features) and in two cases they rebuilt them.

A man smoking hash confessed to me that in Zeewijk, you live in an absence, an amputation. There is a sacrosanct right, for even the poorest of Zeewijk's residents, which is the right of reappropriating scholastic nostalgia, and in great doses at that. It comes from educational institutions, from their soccer fields and their courtyards. Zeewijk's youth—those aged twenty or younger—have lost this right in the sweeping away of both schools and schoolyards. Entire groups of homes and apartment buildings (including the one where I lived when I first arrived) from the reaches of the rings of Saturn have left space for a mineraled spiderweb, an architecture of bourgeois burrows. And, on the subject of Zeewijk's natural rights, what stronger desire could one have, if not the one to outlive the hospital in which they were born? In Zeewijk, many have done even better: the hospital where they were born has died and they have seen another hospital born in its place, one where their six-year-old sons have had their tonsils removed and, if they've been truly lucky, they have seen this hospital demolished, too.

There's a sense of wonder, things to be ashamed of, things that are difficult to share, but if one thinks about it all while he's completely alone at night except for the sobs of a salty wind, he places his head below his quilt and bolts his eyes shut.

One day I told Piet that the Ligurian before him who had sent on a reconnaissance mission to Zeewijk would be content with just one thing: his return to where he was born—that place he loves to call a Ligurian colony—between the walls of a small hospital that then became an old folks home, and to sit there, to be at the same window that heard his first cry and to look on the valley. To be like the old men of Zeewijk, those who outlived the hospitals of their time. Because in our valleys, too—the wide ones in Liguria—things change and become themselves again, but not as drastically. At most, a hospital becomes a shelter: its use changes, but its stones have been there for centuries, its cornices since 1700, chipped and corroded by rains, falling to pieces, and each thing is subject to time's lottery in its own way.

II

Now that Piet is an old man, I realize how time here in Zeewijk is filled to its depths in the same way the alleyways—the *carruggi*—of my home in Liguria are deep.

I haven't worked on the docks for years. I write stories about sand, I go to Piet's regularly, I make my way through the *Calluna vulgaris* and take a currant and bring it to my mouth to eat it until just as I'm about to I see him signal through his window that *no, they are poisonous, even if the lonely sparrows go on eating them.*

Sometimes I don't go in. I stop on the opposite sidewalk and engage in that inveterate habit I've taken up, the gift of a glance through his window.

It's not spying or snooping. Later, I will confess to you what it is.

III

The stories Piet would tell me no longer come to his mind on their own. So, sometimes I remind him myself. First, I read them to him in Italian—he likes the lullaby of my Ligurian, it inspires his smiling nod and half-shuttered eyelids—and then I translate into his language. But these words are broken, and I think that I'll never learn their correct pronunciations.

I remind him of the time he taught me Zeewijk's first rule: Everything changes in Zeewijk, everything except for the streets. Back then I didn't understand. Now, of course, everything is clear. A building that once held lawyers, physiotherapists, and surgeons has become a hotel with a Thai snack bar, a row of storage-units-turned-bike-shops was made from a Turkish-style bazaar that sold all manner of fruits and vegetables, but not the streets. Notice how they conserve their same curves, the original paving stones they started with. It's an exact science: If a stone-paved street suddenly appeared *after the war*, it's still there. Its curbs might change, due process may have added a bicycle lane at the cost of some driving space, the availability of parking spaces might have changed, and its intersections may have been gifted a new roundabout and a speed bump curved like a donkey's back to slow drivers down, in addition to more zebra-striped crosswalks and signs, so even the donkeys bow before the zebras, but the type of paving—the thing that I asked you to pay attention to—has always remained the same. On Piet's suggestion, I went to city hall and consulted the topographical plans of the neighborhood, looking at maps and archival photos of then-asphalted streets. And it was there that I found confirmation, as I did for the bricked streets, each brick laid herringboned against the other until they must be replaced with new ones.

But this rule only applies to the streets, although here and there throughout Zeewijk there are some exceptions. For example, in the span of only a few years the netting made up of the port's piers and canals has become unrecognizable as they have demolished tens of thousands of square meters of stockyards, docks, and warehouses, now occupied by new buildings in an exceptionally Anglo-Saxon style (a choice suggested, no doubt, by tourism since the port hosts ferries to Newcastle and the English like to feel at home even when they're on the continent). Even the names that now appear on the fronts of fish markets are storied ports of England—Dover, Torquay, Leigh-on-Sea. But the paving stones on the streets have remained the same since I worked on the docks.

Why this obsession?

Piet always shrugged his shoulders. According to him, it could be a question of bearings. Some detail must be left the same, so you don't lose yourself among all the new. Otherwise, you would never be able to memorize where anything is since they already change the colors, sounds, and smells. How could anyone guess a street solely by the scent of fish or by the squawking, aerial agony of a seagull's permanent roost if they quickly tear down the building with the fishmonger and evict the seagull? Or learn to curse at a sideways gust of wind if, sooner or later, they block off the path with the beastlike shape of a covered pool in the shape of a kite?

You find your bearings under your feet, Piet says. Your bicycle tire feels the brick or the granular asphalt in such a way that, even with your eyes closed, you could distinguish Siriustraat from the docks at Haring Haven.

IV

My life as a dockworker is of no great importance. We toiled away in cargo holds at temperatures of twenty below, and when I'd arrive home—my apartment in a building they called Dennekoplaan 1 that no longer exists—I couldn't manage to write more than half a page.

For a while, I shared the apartment with a man from Argentina. He was named Pedro, spoke perfect Italian, and was a porn photographer—a *fottografo*, playing on the verb *fottere*, to fuck—until he went to America and left me with an unpaid water bill.

Almost all of us unloading fish were foreigners.

One day, I convinced Piet to try his hand at it—he was still strong as a bull in those days. All bundled up, he followed me on his road bike long before dawn, and he worked for a few hours until, halfway through the morning, he gave up. He couldn't hold up against the cold any longer. He, a Van Bert, a descendent of the very founders of Zeewijk . . . He preferred the humiliation brought on by unemployment checks to Antarctic fatigue.

But there was little fatigue down there because someone set a rhythm, the gift of excessive zeal prescribed by survival. No matter how warmly you dressed, you moved and unloaded boxes of fish or you froze.

I would leave home at five, ride up on my bike, distinguishing the bricked tracts from the asphalt and recognizing the streets even with my eyes closed. Four minutes later, I would slowly descend the fifty-meter incline that led to the docks.

I was greeted by the laughing seagulls, Zeewijk's constant soundtrack, and what rose from the silence the gulls had broken was the asthmatic breath of a monster that lay beyond the canal, a landscape of tall ovens whose fiery tongues would lick at the stars. In that moment, the memory of Liguria was still alive (whereas now it seems to have soaked into the sand) and the mixture of sounds from the steel mill reminded me of the irrigation channels in the country. The sensation of rollers coming up from the subsoil. In Liguria, it wasn't noticeable with many specific places—maybe the stones one might sit upon in the narrow alleyways in front of the church or near the mill, on the old perch that covered the fragmented drains. But in Holland, the iron rodent on the other side of the canal had laid roots everywhere and held the entire sandbar in constant vibration.

I stopped working on the docks when the undeclared overtime did. I'm not the kind for completely legal work. Never have been. In some ways, writing isn't legal work, either.

Or maybe it was that I abandoned the port when it became evident to me that manual labor took too much time away from writing. I noticed that everything drifted by on a ribbon of time set on a dangerous slant, and that ribbon became time that left me no time, or that asked for too much. Simply put, Piet told me one night when we were at his place for dinner, Zeewijk had transformed even me. That must have been it.

V

I left my job in 1992 and returned to Liguria for a few months, to that land I call the colony. Two years had passed since my last visit. The country landscape was marked by a staircase of terraces impenetrable with blackberry brambles.

I spent my days in their shadows, making a place for myself with the quick strikes of a billhook, and waited for nightfall. My mother was still alive then to see me come back to the house bleeding and, if she asked me which field I'd been clearing, I would answer her with a name I had chosen at random: Robavilla, Pozzo, Poggio.

In reality, I was creating a path—at first through the brambles on our property, then trespassing through others—an infestation left carefully intact. My mother was ignorant to all this. Had I confessed it to her, I think she would have been frightened.

From forestry rangers' helicopters above, the countryside must have looked like a jungle now laced with scars that hadn't existed before that summer.

I remained in Italy until September. If I was not amidst the blackberries, I would follow streams, climbing walls of tuff to arrive at springs where I would try to find the sinkholes through which water would escape. My mistake—the same one for all expatriates, exiles, migrants, or, more simply, all fugitives—was scrutinizing the valley to try to remember things, whereas it would have been better to learn it through discovery, to see Liguria as a new land. A colony of Zeewijk . . . That's when I must have begun to think of it that way.

But even if everything seemed all right from inside the blackberry bushes, if I breathed in the rot of time and laid my hands on rusty scythes and abandoned, half-emptied bottles from haymakers who had ended both their thirst and their workdays, if the tiny deaths of snails and rodents hid there, and even if everything were mute and mineralized outside, my relationship with the caretakers in the sandstone village below was irredeemably ruined. They did not expect me and little by little I had become a stranger in a slow process that had begun the moment I left and continued as I stayed away, an erosion I could not protect myself from. When I returned, I was already a stranger—and if I was a stranger to those who had always known me, imagine who I was to those who had only recently arrived to the valley. What had happened in such a short time that no one recognized me anymore?

What did Zeewijk have to do with this? If I asked myself that question, it was because it had become clear to me that my travels to Zeewijk had played a part.

Listen to me, mamma, when I walk—look—grains of sand fall from my pockets. I would have said that to her and I would have scared her, or she would have begged me to find a job.

I had become a writer. That's what had happened. (And that had something to do with Zeewijk.) My name was printed, in full, on the cover of a book. Now, the thing that had always been a fault when I was in Liguria (my curiosity, and moreover my being a *scutizusu*), was legitimized by a back-cover headshot of a thirty-year old with clear eyes and an almost uselessly large brow. I was a writer. The act of writing was not legitimizing, the book was. With a book, you're no longer a busybody, a voyeur, a snoop, and all those improbable, imprecise, incomplete, and inflated words the Italian language has to describe me, only the one in our dialect could hold me like the blackberries held time. *Scutizusu*. The Ligurian dialect succeeded in exporting its voice and its suffixes far and wide, its philological history of Argentine slang rising from the brambles when they were clear, hungry terraces and Ligurian diggers sailed to the docks of Boca from Genoa Rumbo.

A *schena drita*, in the valley's dialect (except for in Civezza and Pietrabruna where a straight back indicates honesty) means someone is lazy. A *fiaccu* is a layabout. They're romantic terms picked up in Buenos Aires. *Squenùn* and *fiacùn*. And there's one more—in some gaucho rosters it still exists—the *scutizusu*. I was *squenùn*, a *fiacùn*, and, above all else, I was a *scutizusu*.

A *scutizusu* is the necessary destiny that precedes the writer: a collector of oddities and a compiler, even in their youth, of imaginary lands, images, and stories. An explorer of private terrains, the *scutizusu* is the boy who asks his father who that land belongs to, how much money their family has, how many olive trees they grow, where the borders of the valley lie, who was a *partigiano* and who wasn't, who had hidden and who had not, who are the dead that I'd seen on the Day of the Dead on their gravestones.

A *scuitzusu* is the boy who dreamed of the Easter festivals to follow the little priest from one village to another, aspergillum in hand, up dark staircases in home after home, fascinated by the secrets of the elderly with their eternally darkened kitchens. The boy who would discover hidden worlds, damp and stinking. He would read in their eyes that they did not want to allow him to see that performance, but he was the one carrying the aspergillum and following the priest, he was the *scutizusu*, the one with a good excuse to see everything and know everything. That boy becomes a writer.

VI

I began thinking about this book a few years ago. I told myself the title would come on its own. After almost thirty years of writing and rewriting the same stories of Ligurian partisan fighters and deserters lost in centuries of Sorba's olive groves, I felt the need to superimpose the Northern grays on the colors of the rainbow. The sands of Zeewijk asked me to. And so, as the geography of my workspace changed—now an old, sturdy metal desk set aside—I decided to let some air into the stories as well. I had bought the metal desk at the Andromedastraat flea market for 65 guilders plus transport. Since it was very heavy, I took it apart and brought it upstairs piece by piece. But two years ago, I discovered that the metal body made my knee stiff and covering my legs didn't suffice since it wouldn't even warm me to twenty-one degrees. My desk now is made of wood.

More than I ever had before, I would take methodical notes of the things I would see during my walks. Even the most normal things. I began to make lists, entirely provisional ones, aware of the fact that time had surely proven me wrong and that, soon enough, hardly anything would be worth admitting in my pages. There was only a handful of buildings destined for a relatively long life, like the Drie Ster—the Three Stars—and the Zeewijkpassage. That was at least what my informants claimed as they gathered to play pool at the *buurthis*—the "Neighbor's House"—and who were also, in some small way, a type of *scutizusu*.

Zeewijkpassage is a true mall. A large depot with parking that dominates the Bellatrixstraat, circled by small shops as if by satellites: the newsstand, the wholesaler, the pharmacy, the wine bar, the florist, the Chinese restaurant. I'd stay there for hours and study the flow, the behaviors of the various fauna: the elderly who loved to shop for groceries early in the morning, the students on a break in their school day, the late-afternoon crowd, and the steady streams of bachelors just before closing, clad in their orange coveralls and rubber boots from other factories, or with their ties and pointed shoes. Women, aloof, in high heels, "beautiful Patagonians" as Piet would call them and, every so often, he would accompany me and have me take note of the details.

He would say: Look, sitting here is just like being at my front window. The one difference was that we were not on a couch, but on some ridiculous circular bench where we had to give ourselves stiff necks in order to speak with each other and it took an entire 180-degree twist of the spine to look at the things that the other pointed out.

Then . . . Then, one day She passed by . . . Her. Do you know what I mean? I pointed Her out to Piet, but he turned too late and almost missed her. Long hair—red—and athletic shoulders and hips and rounded love handles, beautiful and soft like the Ligurian valleys in May.

I asked Piet: What Star do you think she lives on?

Suddenly, her skirt rustled, showing her pale skin, the wind raising an olive leaf and filling its fronds with strokes of light, She passed by and I dreamed of her for a long time . . .

I waited for her to come out with her groceries, but after an hour it was clear that she'd chosen another of the four exits.

VII

In front of Zeewijkpassage, there's a *buurthuis* association that provides all kinds of lessons—singing, music, pool, dance, computer skills—and where they sponsor any type of class one could think up. I go there every so often to have a beer and I'm the kind of person who rarely speaks, someone not very socially integrated they might say only because, in general, the Dutch don't understand me (except for Piet and few others). Or they only pretend to. I've discovered that they pretend.

Not far from the flat *buurthuis* there are the Pleiadean elementary schools and a soccer field named Stormvogels—"storm of birds." The rest could just be called *sand* if you were to remove the constellation of streets and it wouldn't be untrue.

Continuing on the catalog of vignettes that I had begun to curate; one was a study of the different types of buildings and another was on green spaces.

On each apartment block in Zeewijk, in each line of homes soldered to the next, every building is equipped with a dignified piece of manicured greenery, always devoid of benches and divided into zones for children and zones for dogs, the latter marked with a sign—*loslopen honden*, or "dogs allowed," an honest way to euphemistically spell "dog crapper."

The streets of Zeewijk enlace in tessellations and, in accordance with its importance, each receives the name of a star or constellation, a planet or satellite, a nebula. For example, I live on Bellatrixstraat.

Bellatrix is a star in the Orion constellation, found in the Northern Hemisphere. From Earth, Bellatrix is seen easily in winter, except from Antarctica. It's blue and very hot, destined to disappear since it seems to be exhausting its reserve of hydrogen, its nucleus, and now without nuclear reactions it will contract, and its cooling skin will redden within the next million or so years. Now a blue giant, it will become a red giant.

Bellatrixstraat is a brick-laid street, perpendicular to the asphalt beltway called Orionweg, which itself borders many other star-named streets like Betelgeuse (asphalt) and other important streets like Saturnusstraat (asphalt).

Which star did She live on, in which constellation, I'd ask myself each night, my head under my duvet. I couldn't imagine firmament, a window, a yard.

High shoulders, her hands reddened by the cold . . . She was a fishcutter. Did she work at the port? I hadn't gone there for years, how could I meet the women filleting along zinc counters as they laughed and spoke of love like the olive-gatherers of my valley?

VIII

One summer day, many years ago, when Piet was still sprightly and we would go out in the evening to lay out on the grass of the dunes to listen to the frogs, we rested for a long time, hands behind our heads and gazing at the Milky Way.

The idea to give the streets of Zeewijk celestial names was not Piet's father's, urban assessor Willem Leonard, but one of his engineer friends', and his father didn't dislike it.

We lay there, wondering where Bellatrix was and where the Canes Venatici—the Hunting Dogs—were. And after a while, as if inspired by something—some hope or some dream—I remember that I had realized that one day, maybe, a small star would become clear to me from that grand scattered confusion ordered above us . . . I closed my eyes and imagined it, but now I no longer remember . . . But it made me happy to think it might have been Hers.

It was shortly after the crossing of the frogs and the toads. The crossing happens every year, always sometime in May or June, when the frogs travel to give birth in a pond beyond the dangerous Orionweg and, dutifully, volunteers from Zeewijk take to the roadside and stop cars, place frogs in buckets, and transport them to safety.

We lay there listening to frogsong. It was not the thousands of saved frogs that had just given birth to millions of tadpoles, but only one giant frog as she, too, gazed up at the Milky Way.

IX

In the morning, I spend at least a full hour on the circular bench at Zeewijkpassage. My back to the florist, I swivel my head back and forth as if watching a tennis match, trying to see if she will enter through the revolving door to my right or to my left. I have already tried every hour in the morning and, recently, I've started to stop by in the afternoons as well. But she never appears.

Sometimes I get on my bicycle and go to the port. I lock my bike and do the entirety of Haring Haven, the herring pier. I enter the warehouses where they fillet, I climb over heaps of ice, I pass the forklifts and loading zones, I dodge men in rubber boots and white shirts already stained with fish innards, or groups of women who are also in white, always laughing: there goes the guy who's always walking with that man in the hat. I think that's more or less what they always say about me and Piet.

But I don't see her.

In the evening, I lean my bicycle on a lamppost in front of Piet's window, wrap my chain around it, pass through the *Calluna,* and enter his house.

I don't see her at all anymore. For days, I've been looking for her at the market, the port. Nothing.

What was so beautiful about her? What made her so unforgettable? he asks.

Her calves and her back and the fact that she has a short neck and muscles.

X

Zeewijk is a celebration of windows, a world waiting to be anthologized, I say to Piet. But, as such, one is never able to find true happiness there without regretting it.

Piet yawns. He asks me if I've seen her again.

I wish. She's gone.

He's prepared *stampot* and he serves me a plate. Then he asks me to explain to him what I mean about happiness and regret.

I should have been born in Milan, you see, I tell him. In Turin, in Genoa, somewhere where it's possible to pass by unrecognized, not in some small, countryside town where the fate of your own words follows you. Happiness is walking past windows without prejudice, without knowing you're recognized for what you always have been: a *scutizusu*. They've called me a snoop since I was a child.

Piet immediately understood. But sometimes things have to be explained to him from afar, circling the Hunting Dogs, passing through Orion, and coming back out though Aquarius.

When I'd told him that a publisher had asked me to write a book on Holland and I'd decided on the twin styles of Zeewijk's interiors and Liguria's vegetable gardens, Piet crossed his arms and opened his eyes wide. *Het overdreven boek*. That overwritten book. *Het, de.* Articles that I mix up regularly. You have to just know when to use *de* or *het*. There is no feminine or masculine in Dutch; Instead, you have to feel it, you have to have been born there, and it's something like passing by a window and knowing everything at just a glance. One, two, three—three steps with no stopping, no looking around. And with one look you've seen the world being born and dying. You now know Zeewijk's time.

But how do you make an anthology about windows and Ligurian vegetable gardens?

A possible title is—was—*Etchings and Land Registries*. An imitation of Roberto Arlt's *Etchings*. He would go out, observe the street life, the layabouts and loafers, and take notes on everything before returning to his desk at the newspaper to work on them.

To make an etching, you corrode copper with acid. Piet explained this much to me. It's an old form of etching. Then, the images are transferred to paper, then you apply color and the paper is toned and degreased with carbon, before being sprinkled with wax. Then, it's smoked. Finally, it's engraved and, when finally it's inked, it reveals the design. I'll spare you the other, numerous steps because I didn't understand them and, based on how they were explained to me, I'm afraid they weren't very clear to Piet either.

So, you walk by the window, bring everything home, and then your etching begins.

Arlt brought home the vices of Buenos Aires. The full spectrum of layabout—the weak and the loafers, those that *se hace el muerto* (so as to avoid paying their debts). He collected his etchings—his *aguafuertes*—on sidewalks, nothing was private. And that is the difference. I have to enter into homes, capture intimate details. Do I have too strong a conscience? Isn't leaving your curtains wide open already an invitation in itself? I'd say so, and it ends in a trade-off: I look at you in your home, and you look at me as I pass.

Due to this, I feel justified to be a *scutizusu* in Zeewijk.

And now, my own attempt at a gallery of etchings.

Etching 1
   Zeewijk, September 8, 2013, 21:15
   Siriusstraat (House number unimportant)
   First walk-by.
The television is on. From an outside perspective, it's to the left. It's some game show about words, a quiz show with a short name. Near the television stands an orange light, a contrast on the mantle enclosed in a clear lampshade. The walls are bare. On the floor beneath

a light fixture, a dining table with white chairs. Two people sit on the couch—also lit up. A young woman, blonde in a white shirt, and a girl, also blonde and also in a white shirt. They watch TV. Between the table and the window, a young man, standing, papers in his hand as he watches, too. A vase on the windowsill holds a plant with long leaves.

Second walk-by. 21:22.

The man who was standing while watching TV with his papers in hand is missing.

Nighttime walk-by.

All dark. Curtains half-lowered.

I'll try another.

Etching 2

October 22, 16:38

Orionweg (House number unimportant)

No one appears to be home and the objects lining the sill on the other side of the glass make reconnaissance difficult. It's a home belonging to elderly people. What gives it away? The sheer number of objects on the windowsill. The elderly enjoy displaying souvenirs, evidence of a life of short trips to the Ardennes and to Dover, or to Malaga in 1971. The furniture, too, indicates the inhabitants are old. A red-orange light, observed only indirectly, shows a credenza with braided corners, the kind typical of the retro tastes held by the elderly. I'm sure there is thick tablecloth, fringed and with a carpet-like design. The seats, surely worn thin, must have slanting backs. Those are kinds of things that the elderly hold onto until the end. I mean elderly people who are elderly now. They've made it to this point with that furniture and when they pass on, everything they leave behind will never be used again and will end up in the dumpster. The furniture is already older than me and I can clearly remember that I was a child when they were in style. And they seem even older due to the fact that they existed when I was not yet born—and wouldn't be for a good while yet. They were trees that had lived, been cut down, and shaved down in the Fifties, a period that holds the patina of a so-called History. Maybe this furniture was born the same year as the neighborhood and it was the first thing the old people got.

In a short while, they will come home from the grocery, open the door, and the first things they notice will be the smell and the pendulum. The old man will take off his jacket and hang it carefully next to the cabinet as his eye falls on the credenza of braided wood. He will take the bags into the kitchen and leave her to stock the pantry and fridge. He will sit in the living room—on the couch the shade of a discolored sponge or the chair with its wicker armrests—and wait for a tea, a glass of water, and a pill. She won't be long. And as he waits, he will watch their canary jump in its cage, and he will look at the time. Little by little, he'll get used to the smell of his house, meaning here that he'll no longer smell it. For half an hour, he has breathed in the smell of detergent in the mall, the exotic products from the Turkish shop where he bought tea, but the smell of his home had been waiting. Not that he'd ever doubted it. He's home.

In Dutch, house is *huis*, but when you're at home it's *thuis*. It takes just a T to say you're home. The Dutch are home much more than we are, and their language is precise and generous in this. We have other riches. Giuseppe Conte knows the word for every wrinkle of the sea. Francesco Biamonti uses the perfect term for every angle of light and verticality. I think the Dutch women who translate Biamonti must take great pains to find the correct Dutch word for certain terms. In moving to Holland, Piet says, verticality turns to wind.

What else attracts the senses in the home of an old man in Zeewijk, besides the wind outside? The radio—surely, they listen to Noord Holland radio—and the shining objects on the shelf and hung on the walls.

Who knows if Piet knows the old people who live in this home on Orionweg? They aren't much older than him. They're just a bit different, and probably always have been. Piet, for example, doesn't care for woven wicker furniture like other people his age. His furniture comes from secondhand shops, thrift stores, even sometimes from landfills. Piet can't say that there's a man in Zeewijk like him, even if now he's less different from the general population than he was forty years ago. Time smooths and discolors. It makes things the same, and, in the end, it makes everyone a communist, he says.

The old couple has a very well-cared for front garden, and it's naturally very different from Piet's. Based on this garden, the old man appears to be one of those people who puts on a tie every day and participates in city-wide contests to find the best garden in Zeewijk.

Dinnertime walk-by. 18:22.

At the back of the room, light falls on the table and illuminates the old man and woman as they eat. In Holland, dinner is at 6. Due in part to the fact that they're far away, aren't looking at me and sit facing each other, and in part to the fact that they're old and can't see what's happening outside very well, they allow me to continue my investigation undisturbed. There is a pot at the center of the table. Perhaps they prayed before eating, as many of the old, tie-wearing folks in Holland do. Perhaps they're still listening to the radio and there's a warmth in the scent of mashed potatoes and carrots—which the Dutch like—and in the glass of milk that they drink only at dinner. Their knives are used to press the pieces of carrot at the edge of their plates to their forks. Then, passersby approach and I'm forced to follow them, too.

XI

During the month of November, I collected seventy-nine etchings, many retouched through return visits. They are windows into every star and constellation, generally observed after four in the afternoon since that's when their lights are turned on. A particularly beautiful etching is the one of the accordion players in Zwaanstraat: He was in a chair, his fingers on the keys, as if ready to play, but he waited looking out the window. This time, I stopped without hiding my prohibited habit because, in this case, it felt natural—a sign of good manners. It's rude not to stop to listen to someone about to play when he seemed to be waiting for you. I stared at him and he wasn't upset; He returned my smile but decided not to play and stepped away. When I returned, he was no longer there.

And there was that party of young people on some street—I didn't take down the name. Their parents had probably gone out and wouldn't return until late and had left their children as masters of the house. I heard their music from outside, two children jumping and one on the couch with a joint in his mouth, already rolling a second: papers, filter, herb. He realized I'd seen him and invited me to join them, speaking directly to me. At that point, they all looked at me and one of the dancers made a lewd gesture. I moved on, indignant. Something was stuck to all the lampposts lining the street. It read "Wiet Taxi," and there was a phone number. A driving service—legal and taxpaying, I assume—that will deliver marijuana to your home at your call.

And then those families without marijuana or accordions, light blonde children next to their mother as she reads them a story. Sometimes, these children will be blonde for the rest of their lives; other times, no, their blondness slowly takes on the color of wet hay. It goes out like a star.

In one window, adults with a bored stare, and, in the next, a birthday party—no joints, just beers and laughter and more serious drinkers clinking their small glasses of jenever.

And one of those nights, a later one, as I followed my normal route and hid my intentions, my heart jumped into my throat. An extraordinary event.

Zeewijk, November 22, 20:38
Grote Beerstraat (House number unimportant)
Woman, forty years of age, red hair, on the couch. Television on, she is reading a magazine. The couch is black, probably leather, seats three. In front of it, there is an armchair of the same color. Orange-tinted furniture, orange floor lamps, and candles on the small table between the couch and armchair. I can't see her other furniture. I only see her, and I move on just in time as she raises her eyes. Or did she see me?

Second walk-by.
21:40.
She's reading, the television now off. There is a cup on the small table. Was it there before? I stay for no more than an instant; I am certain she has not seen me this time.

General Reconnaissance.
Grote Beerstraat, 22:51.
Some houses have turned off their lights and lowered their curtains. It is the only time of day when residents use the curtains. (Anyone besides those native Dutch—people from Southern Europe or North Africa, Asia or the Slavic nations—tend to hide behind their rolling shutters, electric or powered only by belts and winches, and folding mosquito nets.) At a certain time of night, they think the show is over, turn off the television, and get up from their couches as they wobble with sleep. Glancing at the deserted sidewalk, they lower their curtains, set the room right, bring their cup or glass into the kitchen, check the

doors, turn off the heat and the lights, leaving only one on a very dim setting, and, just before retiring upstairs, they reopen the curtains.

Third walk-by of Her place. 22:53
    . . . to discover she is still reading, the lights still set to the same level, and that the unidentified piece of furniture next to the armchair has a black shelf and a door of orange wood . . . She raises her eyes from her magazine and sees me. She saw me.

XII

She smiled at me, Piet. Of course I'm sure of it . . . No, it wasn't an empty smile. (According to Piet's realism, when someone raises their eyes from a book they automatically smile at the window.)

Her smile is all but empty, and she has very intelligent eyes, which she raised, and I bet she wouldn't have smiled but she saw me, and she did. Then she came to the window with those athletic shoulders supporting her neck and she smiled again. I couldn't see her calves. I would have liked to see her walk, as she did at Zeewijkpassage.

And I want to know her name, Piet.

Ask her. Write on a piece of paper in printed letters: My name is Marino Magliani, writer and translator from the Spanish, I'm Italian, from Liguria, you? and then stand beneath the lamppost with that paper, and she'll come to the window to read it. One time you told me about that Pablo d'Ors book—the one with that man who talks to the woman he loves on the phone, but he's never seen her. He doesn't know her name, she's simply a voice that calls him every day at 6:30 in the evening and asks him if he's ready, because his only job in that little train station is to lower the barrier at 7 when the train passes. And, in the end, after having heard her voice every day at 6:30 with the same beautiful question—"Ready?" or "All set?"—he has fallen in love.

XIII

The idea is to spend as little time as possible with the Ligurian part—cold, synthesized descriptions and the reader should have the impression they are reading a land registration report. The first notice refers to the Map Layout. Each Layout, as best as I remember, is assigned a Roman numeral. Then the Parcel, Lot, and Quality of Terrain—the type of agricultural macroculture attributed to that specific terrain. Then, Class—the level of productivity—and then there's *ha*—surface (hectares)—and *are*—surface (ares). Then, Weekly Income, the typical average income from agricultural activity, and Agricultural Yield, the part of said income attributable to the working capital and labor engaged, considering the land's potential and limitations. But how can it be done? In Liguria, things are measured differently. Names are the land's biography.

Vallonello, Gilun, Fanga, Ciazze, Poggio, Gianchin, San Luca, Salita del Soldato. These are where forfeitures play out. Income is the product of a careful equation, a quantity yielded by a chemical reaction in which the coefficients are memory and kinship.

Let's put it like this: There are lands that I love for their objective and untamed beauty, rocks that absorb sunsets, trees in refreshing shadow, etc., and there are lands aesthetically insignificant but otherwise immense that tell the story of a boy who has not yet escaped them.

Vallonello Vegetable Garden. Municipality: Sorba.
    Layout X
    Parcel 386
    m sq. 890
    Quality: meadow

Vallonello is called that because it has the shape of a valley, ignoring all the reasons why it is classified as a meadow. For us, it was the garden below the houses. The morning sun didn't reach them before ten. This vegetable garden was on the last of the terraced steps. It was bordered by canebrake and, further downstream, a wall of cut stones of varying heights rested on the riverbed like rows of teeth. The stones, even those at the very top of the wall, showed signs of algae left by memorable winter floods.

There were two persimmon trees in Vallonello and straight furrows of beans, marked lengthwise in the way my father preferred. Not even a single row of nostralina olives, and too much dew and too little sun for a vineyard. You could look up at the houses from there. I can count the terraces from memory alone. There were twelve terraces about ten meters deep, each divided by the mule path of steps that led to asphalt.

I remember an old man, the owner of one of these vegetable gardens, who used to send me to the fountain to get water. And another old man who tended the garden with who I thought was his wife, who I later discovered to be his mother. The old man with the fake wife one day asked me, Have you ever seen a mole? No, I replied. I ran to the spot. He had killed it with a hoe, a drop of blood trickled out its nose. They're a plague, the old man said. They ruin everything, said his fake wife.

I knew that they were ceaselessly digging, and it seemed like their right since they lived down there. The moles had a relationship with earth like humans have with water. If I went down to the river and put my head below water, I could stay like that for a little bit of time, but then I had to breathe. That's also how it was for the moles, who were able to remain below ground for as long as days but needed to come up sooner or later and then the old man quickly found them and delivered the fatal blow. Thwack, a single strike, he said, mimicking the descent of the hoe. The moles were too blind to see Death and, instead, died instantly, before being picked up by their rat-like tails and launched across my garden, ending up on the gravel riverbank or in the water.

I was unhappy that, in death, they didn't return to the places they'd loved in life. That humans were the ones who went underground instead, that they were the ones I'd never see again and who abandoned their fields and the streets, their walking paths outside, the lines in shops and the fountain. The old man with the fake wife, she herself, and even dozens of others, all alone as I am now, would one day take the place of the murdered moles. Once I accompanied the priest in a black surplice with an aspergillum, as if I were a little priest-in-waiting, and we followed the crowd—they, too, behind the pallbearers with their box. We stopped for at least half an hour in the cemetery and when we went to leave, single file, the old man who had died stayed behind. He was underground and, every so often, like the moles, he would come up to breathe.

He's underground, I would tell myself while I walked back into town with the priest, but he isn't down there forever. Every so often, his head will pop out, like it used to do when he would dive underwater when he was little. He'll look around, breathe, and go back down before he's struck with a hoe.

Maybe there are moles in Zeewijk, too. They make holes in the sand, dig out entire floors and passageways, gnaw on pipes and cause sinkholes under the brick and asphalt of various streets. I often stop to watch the excavators at construction sites, the operators with their neon uniforms and square shovels, the kind you use for sand. I stay there until they ask if everything's okay. And were I to ask them, very seriously, "Have you seen any moles?" they would laugh, when it's no laughing matter at all.

Mol. That's how you say it in Dutch. From de-*mol*-ish, I would assume. *Mol,* which must be masculine. Unlike the Italian *talpa.*

Gilun. Municipality: Sorba.
  Layout X
  Parcel 479
  m sq. 398

Quality: field
Class: unique
Weekly Income and Agricultural Yield: unclear

To get to the *Gilun* garden, you had to go down to the Case Sottane and cross the Roman bridge. Other than that, there wasn't a true or correct path, and you had to balance on the edge of the irrigation duct, which we call a *bealera* in the valley.

It was one of the first fields we abandoned. The income equations don't work here, the yield calculated in beauty and allocated by the memories it provides. There's too much missing data. I would sit on the edge of the *bealera* and look out across the river, where the new bridge on the county road climbed uphill. *Gilun* is like a window; Stay, see who passes on the bridge, and watch as they look back at you.

Fanga.

I don't have access to this land register. Like its name in Italian suggests, it truly was just *mud*. It was always a flooded, karstic territory situated between rustling reeds and the cries of beasts in the shadows. The street ran beneath the terraces. One day, maybe to see what would happen—even though, today, I'm not sure that was why at all—I picked up a handful of gravel and threw it against the body of a blue Seicento. The driver slammed the brakes. My mother ran up and made me apologize immediately. I still don't know why I did it, but, given the name of the location, one could say that I pulled myself up out of it somehow.

Robavilla. Municipality: Gansia.
 Layout XXIX
 Parcel 86
 m sq. 7200

Quality: olive grove
Class: unique
Weekly Income and Agricultural Yield: unclear.
Notes: Chronicle of a Half Orgasm caused by a Vegetable Machine

I was fourteen years old and I suffered from vertigo. When I would climb the olive trees, I would never go beyond the lowest branches; Any higher and I'd begin to shake and immediately fall. Maximum ascent: 3 meters. This is to say that my elapsed time of descent, always hugging the trunk, was very short. This was enough, however, a brilliant day—my feet again on the ground—for me to remain for a brief moment embracing that trunk, so gentle to have caused me to ejaculate. In Robavilla, the calculations of agricultural yield rise, too.

XIV

Zeewijk.

From November 28 to December 3, I passed through Grote Beerstraat—
the Great Bear—at least twice a day, almost always between 5:00 and
7:45 in the evening.

First contact was made November 30, between 5:00 and 5:15. I
was afraid I was invisible. But she noticed me, and she smiled at me.
I pulled out the paper with the Dutch sentence Piet dictated to me,
the translation of which I provide below:

My name is Marino Magliani, I'm Italian, and you?

But the lamplight isn't exceptionally bright, she can't read it, and
she motions for me to cross the thirty centimeters of wall between us
and press the page to the window.

I obey, approach the window, bow halfway, and can almost smell
her perfume through the glass.

She reads and returns with her own piece of paper, putting it to
the window. There, she's written:

Ik ben Anneke, nederlandse. She is Anneke, Dutch.

November 30, around 6. I run to her house, another paper, one I
translated myself without Piet. It's fine.

Me: I'm a translator and a writer, you?

Her: I fillet herring and sole.

I figured.

December 1. I had already passed by once, but she wasn't there, so I come back after 5. From then on, I notice that she's always there. She rushes to the window. I ask her permission to do the same.

Message translated by Piet, again translated here:

Me: In Italy, I live somewhere that looks out on the sea, which is green and you can even see the bottom.

Her, after returning with paper and pen:

I used to live in Mercuriusstraat.

19:00

Me: I had dinner, prepackaged salad and herring. You?

Her: Cherry tomatoes and rice, sole, apple. *Lekker.*

(Which means "good." The Dutch overuse the term *lekker.*)

I pull my papers from my jacket pocket and search for one. (Piet translated around thirty sentences for me, a handheld potpourri of phrases the quality of which I benefit greatly from.) I move closer.

Me: I'm going to the beach tomorrow. I think that it will be windy.

Her (She takes less than a second to write in block letters. She has a beautiful neck.): I'm going to bed soon.

XV

Ask for her last name, Piet told me.

And I had hoped that she would have introduced herself by first and last name. I could simply read the last name on the brass nameplate below her doorbell located just on the other side of the door, but the window is a couple meters away from it and I would have to exit the front garden to take the brick path, or I would have to climb the hulking cascade of plants and northern ferns in order to reach it.

I could check her last name during the day when she's not there, but it doesn't seem right for me to approach without her permission. I'd be afraid her neighbors might say something. So, I stick to our rules. I only press my piece of paper to the window when she notices me, smiles, and makes that gesture with her hand. The first time I didn't wait, I thought she was asking me what I wanted from her. I thought, What a character! We're off to a good start! Then I understood. She wasn't irritated at all, it's that through lip movements and mime that she was trying to ask who I was.

December 2, 2013, I returned to Piet with the news: I'd seen her again at the market. I wasn't on that circular bench, I was shopping, I was by the produce, over by the thirty or so varieties of Dutch potatoes. She passed me and smiled. I said, "Good day," and she responded with "Good afternoon." I must confess that I would have preferred never to hear her voice. It would have been beautiful to keep talking about her in this book without ever having known her voice.

The flâneur passed in front of the window, in love, and spoke by showing her his pages, I said to Piet.

Piet thought while he translated more of my phrases, then stopped himself, lifting his eyes and saying: Again, it's almost like the d'Ors book—actually, it's like its opposite. In the adventures d'Ors wrote, the narrator fell in love with a woman without ever having seen her, and having only heard her voice.

Here, I transcribe the rest of my conversation with Anneke with complete fidelity.

Me: You don't say "Good afternoon" in Italian, even if it is so beautiful to say. It's just—you never know if afternoon is over at six or seven. Nowadays, when it's dark by four, it's even more difficult to tell where the border is.

And she . . .? Piet asked.

She said *ehh*. So, I sought the correct words in Dutch and explained to her that it's like colors. Try, if you can—I told her—to tell Zeewijk's gray from others. She looked at me and tilted her head.

Take now, for example, I continued. Is it afternoon or already evening?

And she . . .? Piet wanted to know.

She nothing. She smiled, her head tilted in the same way it does when she writes on her own pages, said it was still afternoon, and she left.

XVI

They say that even the chlorophyll is gray here. The houses are brown brick, or else they'd be gray, too. The sunlight in the fields and groves of Liguria is fair compensation for the gray one finds in Zeewijk, I tell Piet.

No, he returns. Sunlight is on your vegetable gardens. Zeewijk's light is the moon coming in through the window.

Great intuition, Pietro, that must be why I always decide to take my walks as darkness falls. Drops of light from half-moon shaped lamps—moonlight on earth, oranged or yellowed—from walls, candles as affected as the walks they light.

We're at his house, sitting on the sofa. He uses a classic style of lighting, a lamp hanging from the ceiling—one that has watched over him for years as he reads—and a neon light in the kitchen.

I look at the oblique slice of light through the window's crust. Once a year, the Saturday before Pentecost—I'll explain why later—Piet washes his window. So, for at least a month I can watch those who pass outside. But if I approach it now, it isn't until I'm very close that I can do so through the patina of salt. The man with his hands in his pockets, for example, or the mother with her groceries in one hand and her son's hand in the other. The mother who walks her bike like a dog on a leash; I assume she's a mother because of the child's seat mounted on her handlebars.

I talk to Piet about it. People don't thirst to look into your window. They walk on, always looking straight ahead, passing by and ignoring you.

Do you look into windows thirstily?

Always, I respond. It's a ritual.

And, sure, the reaction of those I observe has, more than once, been a face that seems to say, So what? Since I'm prone to feeling guilty, I don't pass the same window twice in a short amount of time. I always make a long trip. I walk down Cassiopeia, turn towards Orionweg and follow the left-hand sidewalk—the one with odd numbers, buildings on the right.

I watch, confronting another hundred windows, until I finally dare to retrace my steps. I pay close attention and then, with any luck, I find a new scene, new people seated, a father in the place of his daughter and a PSV Eindhoven game instead of an MTV show. Or I look in the window again to find no one this time. Everything off, except one light to guard against thieves, because they know to beware of those.

It's not uncommon, however, to be presented with the same exact scene, the television still on and the same fauna as before: children rapt in images, a mother in her nightgown—the beautiful worn-in kind—and a father in the recliner, armed with a beer.

Even I used to like walking along the streets, Piet confessed. But no one ever came out to say "So what?" to me.

Do you think that they knew you were watching them? I asked.

He doesn't think so. His theory is that the man passing by us at that very same moment with something like a leash in his hand (our view from the window cuts off the dog) is watching us intensely, whereas we only see an apathetic glance.

These things can't be verified at my house—Piet knows—because Bellatrixstraat is home to *maisonette* apartments. I live on the second floor and in order to see the sidewalk I have to stand up and move to the window. Then, of course, I can see who is passing by and the passerby can see me and the window and nothing else, but if I step back, they see only my window and the ceiling. For this reason, I walk straight ahead when I see windows stacked high like those in Bellatrix.

For *maisonettes*, a soundproofing system of floors is expected. On the second floor, I have a living room, kitchen, and toilet. On the third, I have the shower, the room where I write and the one where I sleep. The tenant above me has the rooms above mine and to get to his kitchen, living room, and toilet, he must go upstairs, and the tenant above him has a layout like mine. Because of this, we don't disturb one another. When I write or sleep, my upstairs neighbor might be writing or sleeping, and when I'm at my living room window, my alter ego below me doesn't exist since I live on the lowest floor and maybe that means that alter ego is the man passing by on the street, maybe he's the one who comes before me.

Piet has always suggested I get a puppy. You're noticeable if you go out at night without a dog. In Zeewijk, the people who go out like that have dogs. A dog is a justification. You have the dog, and so you can wait three minutes in front of a window (as long as you show your waste bags as necessary). No one will ever notice that it's not the dog who pulls you, but the other way around. And when you have a dog on a leash, who would ever suspect why you'd already passed three times? But I'll come back to this later, too.

The fact is, with my obsession with these domestic interiors, I lose the effect the view of a front garden has. Some people dress them with perfectly manicured horizontal hedges and are always present, cutting them down with their shears. These hedges permit one opening onto the sidewalk, a singular connection between resident and passerby— no interference, no distraction, but a constant guard to be aware of, who protects at least one person on the far side watching the pathway. It doesn't matter if he's distracted, he stands behind that glass and pretends to do what he must. When he's alone, it can be a difficult duty; He reads his book and stands guard, watches TV and stands guard, naps on the couch and stands guard. However, when he's on the couch, or in an armchair, or on his feet, there's an entire squadron; It's a changing of the guard.

It's not always exactly so, but the passerby's anxiety and fear of being caught can overtake reality.

Others don't take up hedgework, but if that's the case then they must be in agreement with their neighbors, or else it's useless for number 21 not to have hedges when 19 and 23 do.

Within the last few years, almost all residents have covered the sand in their front yards with a kind of peat. The mixture creates striking results, *Cotinus coggygria* grows—the *Young Lady* genus judging by the bronzed and iron-colored leaves. *Hydrangea Butterfly*, or the glaucous perennial *Sedum matrona*, and all kinds and colors of the *Cupressaceae*—junipers.

The Dutch love to be asked about their front gardens. If the plants have Latin names, they are sure to use them as the Dutch love using Latin, even in their Gregorian chants. When this happens, I find myself asking the name of those strange trees with the leaves like plastic and why there's a taste for a fundamentalist pruning that forces the plants into unnatural, triangular shapes, some tied in rows of vines and others rounded like snowmen. It's an obsession, the amputation and strangling of plants.

For me, these situations are ideal. While we talk botany, I look inside their homes. However, these situations are still dangerous because these people remember me after we talk a little and, whenever I pass again, I fear they will recognize me and raise their hand in hello.

Oh, that's the man who complimented my tulips . . .

There are other encounters that leave no trace—ones that happen other places—which is to say that I am not recognized after. For example, Sundays, in church. We share the same pew with devoted familiarity, even if I am not recognized on the street. In reality, yes, I recognize everyone—man and woman—when they see me again, be it on the street or in the woods or at the supermarket. I'm tempted to nod slightly, to say Good afternoon, or simply lift my hand, but I doubt that the gesture would be returned. They would react with a forced greeting based in manners, not given because I was recognized as the man who was at Mass.

The true Magliani, Piet insists, can be distinguished from the Magliani *scotizozo*. (He would always say it with two Z's.)

XVII

I didn't see her again for four days. I would approach Grote Beerstraat, hopeful, but her lights were off. I passed by during the day. Nothing.

December 5 was better: Anneke was home and she smiled at me. I had a sheet of paper with me:

Anneke, the last time I went to the beach, the tide had just beached the starfish and crabs. Hundreds of starfish. Maybe they were waiting for the tide to take them out again.

I took it out of my pocket, showed it to her. But she made no sign she cared to read, and, without her permission, I didn't have the courage to cross the ferns and press the page to the window. I folded it up, waited on the sidewalk for a few moments, and then continued my walk.

December 5 is Sint Klaas, the children's holiday. I always leave my home with something like excitement, sure to find generous windowscapes: scenes of applauding people, children who jumping among unwrapped gifts, family reunions. Someone passes by, looks until he's sated, and no one takes notice of him.

XVIII

Piet never comes to Sunday morning Mass. There's a Catholic Church on Zuiderkruisstraat (the Southern Cross, a minuscule constellation near the feet of the Centaur). Service begins at ten and ends at eleven. The organist is an old man, but very alert, slight, full of energy. Outside of church, I see him three times a week at the gym. Both of us commit to a little cardio a safe distance away from the people with tattoos and bloated biceps who frown as they lift enormous weights. Then it's not uncommon for us to see each other again in the sauna. Twelve square meters, four benches—two raised—a timer and a basin of water, eucalyptus to use with great caution. From the glass door, you can see the changing area.

I disobey most of the rules and bathe the scalding stones with a lot of eucalyptus, then lay down, close my eyes, and start to think of strange things. For example, I imagine the houses in Zeewijk if they, too, were all equipped with saunas (even the organist has his own passionate dreams behind tightly-shut eyes, I suppose) and video cameras that check the window traffic, that register how many times the same person passes by, if he was alone, and other similar details, and these things are signaled to the resident only when he is in the sauna, which has a video system to be cleaned from time to time so the screen doesn't cloud over.

XIX

Zeewijk, December 7, 2013
Grote Beerstraat, around 18:00.

She's eating dinner, alone, at the end of the room, where the Dutch typically place their tables so as to look out at their back garden while they eat their meal.

She sees me and smiles; I smile as well and continue on.

I think she got up and ran to the window at that exact moment. I say that because, upon my return after only a few minutes, I find her waiting, her hand on the window.

She has a sheet of paper in her hand, holds it to the glass, allows me to read it, and takes it down.

I run to Piet, down Ursa Major, onto Jupiterstraat, to the right when it ends, then along Steenbok (our magical Capricorn), under glistening trees, lighted garlands, and the narrow streets that scream with light. I cross Eenhoorstraat Plaza (also known as Giacomo Sartori's Unicorn, the one that lives only when I open its book) and pass behind Bellatrixstraat without stopping. People turn to look at me, and the children who thought I was lazy and slothlike and who have never seen me run stop playing soccer and begin to clap. Leashed dogs bark at me. I make it to Piet's, exhausted.

She wants to read something I wrote. Don't you see? That's what she wrote on that paper. That's something!

Piet sends me to fill the pitcher with water. When I return, he has the stupidest idea that he has ever had. Why not give her your book, the one that's been translated into Dutch?

Piet, do you understand what you're proposing? A book full of muddied words, written at a time when I shared a home with that man who took those pictures and spoke only of *doggy* and *rubbers*, as he would put them. A romance, sure, but something too bestial. No, it needs to be softer, something that slowly lowers the shutters that are her eyelids so she can understand that I am a dreamer, pure and lyrical, a stupendous and rare example of regal marginality . . .

I have to write what I want her to read.

I leave Piet's after a few hours, half-happy. We're in agreement; I'll stop by to pick up the translation tomorrow. I wrote a few pages, first in Italian, then in my approximate Dutch—a language *ad personam* that Piet knows well—and tomorrow morning he will work on it, set everything right.

I wander in the thick air, calling forth sleep. Every time I think I know what awaits me, what I know by heart, I'm surprised when I turn Orion's corner and the shock of the North Sea's icy whip finds me like it did thirty years ago, and I falter. There are two types of wind, the kind that passes silently and the kind that announces itself—the first moves you with malice, the other is only a voice.

With my collar up and my hands in my pockets, I pass darkened windows. The right thing to do would be to hurry to the dunes or to make my way home . . . But I can't resist, so I look for a place that, at least, has no lampposts.

In the process, I pee on the Plutostraat's majestic poplar. Naturally, I hear steps behind me, followed by smaller steps that scratch at the sidewalk.

Is that a way to act at your age, the Dutchman says as he and his dog stop beside me. I had almost finished.

I shake, adjust the crotch of my pants and zip them, then dry my hands on my jacket. I turn and kindly greet the gentleman in his language. Look, I tell him, you're right, but I couldn't wait any longer and then I would have had to use the phrase that we use in my valley—trust me, that's worse—because in situations like these, we say: Dear sir, with this bird in hand, I can piss in any bush.

The man insults me, and the dog does, too.

XX

Zeewijk isn't divided up by how chic its neighborhoods are now, but instead into chic and less chic periods. Take Planetenweg, for example: the backbone that connects the constellations. It's the street that I take to get to the gym, my cap crushed to my ears and my black gym bag slung over my shoulder. I sail along the coast of four exceptionally long buildings, the oldest of which—an accordion-styled building from the seventies—was swept away last year to rebuild the same exact building in its place with only one difference: new materials, meaning higher prices to rent or buy.

Every day on my journey with my gym bag on my shoulder, I pass the lady Diana's *Viskraam*, a fried-food cart of incredible fish and anchovies. Then, I pass by the *buurthuis*, the apartment block placed almost perfectly as an impediment to car traffic—in fact, they call it *de Dwarsligger*, "The Obstacle." There, people play billiards and take lessons in dance and painting. I've taken all their courses, including Arabic and German, a course on how to use power drills, and one on Mexican cooking. Having rounded the Obstacle, a long, new four-story accordion is presented on my left. This part of town is chic and, until last year, was a place that rented to young students, workers, retired people with little means, and the unemployed; now there are SUVs parked at the trellis where they would tie their bicycles. In ten years, they'll tear down what's now the low-popular part of Planentenweg and in forty years they'll substitute the accordion that, forty years earlier at that point, had been newly built.

The eye gets used to new lights; Where there used to be a full room of screaming and trembling color, a *Zeepunk* rumble of Nordic metal bands, you're now lost in an unfocused penumbra of sophisticated and serious women crouched over their laptops, rampant young men and women eating dinner by candlelight, kitchens with electric stovetops and modern ovens, crystal objects. The eye remembers, connects vices and habits, collects art objects.

For the past two weeks, the eye has seen a man in the corner apartment of the accordion, always on his feet, serious and perhaps melancholy, and high up, in the window, a rectangular poster with the name of a real estate agency and the words *Te KOOP*. "For sale."

What happened? Why doesn't this unmarried man (the eye knows all) who doesn't live with a partner (either male or female) and does not yet receive visits from children or others and has no dog and no bicycle—how, after three months of living in the brand-new accordion on Planetenweg, has he come to the decision to sell?

Did he not know the neighborhood, and is he worried about it now? Did he happen to get the worst neighbors? Has he only now realized that he can't pay the mortgage? No matter, the eye doesn't care to know all this. As it has gotten used to him, it will get used to the next owner, and sometimes it will even miss the old one.

"Mortgage," in Dutch, is *hypotheek*. But you don't mortgage anything here. The large part of the residents in these apartments have a good job, with which the bank calculates a monthly payment. Here, they don't sell from vegetable gardens like Ligurians, nor do they have rural buildings to pass off as urban ones in order to rent them to Germans on vacation. Here, they don't even own the sand on which their homes stand. The two hundred meters of sand between their living room and their garden will always belong to the City. They're fixed-term owners. Why can't the City afford to lose its right to modify the town plan? Dispossessing an area takes what they think is too long. Nevertheless, the housing corporations aren't too bad, and rent is paid in proportion to one's income. There's a roof, subsidized for those who sleep under it. This is the syndrome of poverty. Sometimes, it isn't worth earning an extra hundred Euro a month if you'll lose the subsidy.

The *te koop* or *te huur*—"for rent"—posters stay up for months, a year. Then, after just one night, you'll pass by the window and find it empty, cleared of lamps and furniture, wallpaper removed despite how new it was, the wood or carpeted floor now bare—an empty stall. They get a new job and they move; They lose it and become content with a less expensive home. Here, there's steel and there's fishing, a pleasant scent of fried eels and herring, the coming and going of refrigerated trucks, of people with rubber boots and shirts that are always dirtied with fish blood. Sailors with black clogs and wool berets, their hobby crafting wooden models of ships that they exhibit in the windows. They're men in blue with untamed beards and already faded tattoos, and they stand in front of the windows, their legs wide as if they were trawling in the middle of the North Sea.

The empty houses take new tenants, someone goes out to exercise and passes with his black gym bag and discovers the window bright with new tenants as they paint the walls white and paste wallpaper, make holes to hang posters of beaches with white sand or paintings with fishing scenes from another century or Hals imitations, a moving truck taking up the whole sidewalk, piles of garbage, carpet swatches.

You pass by, and from that moment you'll become their point of view, even if they'll never recognize you.

XXI

Zeewijk
  December 8, about 18:00.

Grote Beerstraat is an exaggerated celebration of Christmas.

I wait on the sidewalk on the other side of the street, make sure that she sees me, and, with great hope, I show her my sheet of paper. She smiles and, again, makes that gesture that I hadn't understood in the beginning—interpreted as "who are you and what do you want" and, instead, an invitation.

I cross Ursa Major to her sidewalk, I cross the thirty centimeters of wall, I cross the gravel that screeches beneath me. I pull tape and scissors from my jacket pocket, cut two pieces, and hang my page on the window.

The translation I'd picked up this afternoon. Piet says he's satisfied with it. Of course, I would have liked for her to read the original, which I reproduce here and trust more, but I didn't tell Piet that.

Sunset

Anneke, those who live deep in the wide valleys of my youth soon learn to raise their eyes to fire. Watching the sun set is one of the first things a child does in Liguria.

Our valleys are grottoes, Anneke; Light enters from only one point—an escape in the morning and afternoon—and, in the evening, a tiny piece of sky hosts daylight with great difficulty—a light blue cage, as Vincenzo Pardini writes. In that light, they say you can feel the sea.

Not in the light itself, Anneke, but in what draws it to the moon. Like the cliff confronting the countryside. I had to see it from the West, and the more I looked at it, the sadder I was, even if I liked what I was looking at, even if it was like looking at you. That's why it made me sad. At sunset, the valley was too beautiful, but I had thought this and said this before, even if, when tourists arrived in the valley, I would ask myself what beauty they could find here that Germany lacked. Germany must have no open cliffs baked by the changing seasons, and no terraces where nothing grows in time and where fire consumes the young greenery and crumbles the sandstone. Germans liked these landscapes; They stood looking at them for hours and I didn't understand why. Now, I know they did it so they could drink a bottle of wine.

You can only view the valley in sunset from the shadows, from "the other side," a world exhausted despite man's interventions: metal netting and blocks of sandstone and Colombina stone which don't crumble but, instead, fall apart in the grill.

Looking at the cliffs from "the other side," the sun fell at my back. The day commanded the line of shadow—long and well-ordered like an army's cavalcade—that crossed the stream and climbed the terraces. In order to see the place where day sank down, you had to follow the mule paths, cross the stream and the asphalt that ran alongside it, and re-climb the rocks on the east side and stop at a certain point, before it was late, turn to look at the hinge holds the Val Prino closed. Then, stay there, at that one point of surrender which is still nothing yet because, on this side of the world, the light always forgets her bright-purpled rags.

It was the time when swifts sang—they don't fly there but madly move about with open beaks so as not to miss a single gnat—maddened, grazing at the edges of our land and at the reeds—at the bottom, at the very bottom of things where the streams meet and where night has already fallen.

In other seasons, the light's edge lasted much shorter and the robin quickly closed the gates of the day.

During winter, Liguria becomes a grotto even before gaining moonlight and the darkness invades even sleep.

XXII

There are days, especially now when it's snowing, when Piet and I spend our time sitting on the circular bench inside the mall. Camouflaged amidst the vegetables of an exotic garden of plastic, we sit and watch the hustle and bustle of the residents of Zeewijk as they take their carts, enter, do their shopping, exit, leave their carts.

We know the overwhelming majority of these people; We know where they live, when they eat dinner, what they watch on television. If they buy the potatoes from the blue pickup truck on Tuesdays between 4 and 7 in the evening, I know it. (It's blue, no sideboards, and a man dressed like a janitor drives it, stops in front of his clients' houses, takes down the 25-kilo sack, puts it on their bill, and leaves.) I know everything, including who's subscribed to the *Top Tuin N.H*, "The Best Gardens of North Holland," and who gets a magazine dropped in their mail slot every Thursday by the boy with the bag hanging from his bike.

If the residents of Zeewijk have a son or daughter that does karate two nights a week, the child leaves with their white gi, crosses the street, traverses Sirius, cuts through Bellatrix, avoids the obstacle of the *buurthuis*, and enters the karate and judo dojo. Sometimes I pass by and pause in the doorway, waiting for one of the shouts in Japanese or Chinese that are yelled like an alarm, and then the sound of backs falling on mats.

At first, I had registered for a course on using nunchaku—that weapon made of two sticks of wood connected by a chain that, if someone becomes half-good at it, can hit a dozen people. There was a night school for photography nearby. I registered for that, too, entering one door and exiting the other at midnight. Then, I put down roots at the latter; I halted my payments and returned my gi and rubber nunchaku.

The library is the one thing I still pay for. It's there that I'd heard talk of Fonds van Letteren, some kind of writers' syndicate. It looks for quality—that's what's written on their site, even if they lack an explanation of how it's calculated. Marketability, however, isn't important. This calmed me. I spoke with some Dutch writers and naturalized Dutchmen, as well as some foreign residents in Holland who wrote in their mother tongue as I did and who had been published in their countries. I knew a Pakistani man who had presented a beautiful project to Fonds: a series of novels on the secondary, unknown silk roads. They paid a translator and took it upon themselves to find a publisher. Which they did. The Pakistani man received what they call a *beurs*, which means a whole lot of money.

I enthusiastically presented myself, the false disciple of regal marginality, at Fonds. I said that I lived alone on a rainy coast ten months of the year and wrote novels that were shored up (as I was, too) between the horizontal Holland and vertical Liguria. In Italy, the novels had inspired the interest of both great publishers and great critics. Soon, however, I was aware that I didn't enter into the sustainable category. I was not a writer from Holland who wrote in Dutch, nor was I a non-Western writer like the Pakistani man who wrote in ancient Sindhi jargon. I was non-Dutch, and a non-non-Westerner. I was an Italian and publishers from Holland were full of Italian books—there were great translators from the Italian, and scouts and agents.

The interest in translating my books into the language of the Netherlands came when I least expected it. One day, while I was in Italy—among the brambles—I received a telephone call from my agent. A pair of Amsterdam publishers, one of whom was very well-known, had bought the rights to two of my books. From that day on, I had a translator on my heels.

Sometime after the first book came out, a young woman appeared on Bellatrixstraat for an interview. She said she worked for the most fashionable Dutch arts and culture magazine. She herself was very fashionable. She said that the publisher didn't have my contact information and she was right: I didn't have a telephone and had never responded to their emails because the computer was broken. We spoke on the sofa, she would occasionally throw back her head in something like a tic, and then we walked the sidereal streets of Zeewijk. She had brought a photographer with her who, every so often, would suddenly take pictures of me—his own tic. I successfully convinced them that we should take some shots outside Zeewijk, out near the World War II bunkers where you could see the sea.

The interview came out under the title *Fated to Wander*. And there I was, a piece of paper in hand as I looked out to the horizon with the air of someone who might, in fact, be fated to wander. A four-page report. And there were beautiful reviews in the most important newspapers. They praised the doubling of my sun-moon pairing, Ligurian vegetable gardens-Dutch interiors. Then, a very shrewd and wealthy publisher came, and made me a scandalous proposal: A book on the places I'd claimed to have lived—Argentina, Norway, Chile, Spain, a lot of Spain, a lot of Costa Brava. He wanted to know what I'd done in Costa Brava, by way of his interpreter since he was convinced he couldn't understand my Dutch.

Nothing, I said. In Spain, I'd slept under an upturned boat, and then I translated the menus for all the restaurants in Costa Brava from Spanish into Italian and slept an entire summer in a boarding house where, in bed at night, I'd hear the static of the sea which only served to remind me of when I had slept under the boat. The interpreter stammered and had me repeat myself. Nothing, just loser things and nothing with a hook. The shrewd publisher used the word "hook" in every sentence and gestured with his index finger as if pulling a trigger. *No me gustan los perdedores*, there's no hook, he said so we could understand how well-versed he was in multiple languages. His publishing house translated cult Chileans, Spaniards, Mexicans, some of the best-selling Italians.

Something violent, he suggested. There needs to be a story with a lot of sex appeal.

Sex? No, I admitted. Very little sex. I was a watcher—but I didn't watch those who would have sex at night near the overturned boat and wouldn't let me sleep. I was more interested in watching life, *en passant*, in that small town full of tourists and the non-places in the 80's on the Costa Brava. The shrewd and wealthy publisher was convinced that sex was the hook; He gave me some money and convinced me to write a book about sex on the Costa Brava. In truth, I had already had an outline of some kind of travelogue. I would change it in order to accommodate a sexual plot and call it *The Beach of Romantic Dogs*—an homage to Roberto Bolaño's poems—the translation of which would become *Het strand van de romantische honden*. Then, I shopped the Italian text around Italy. I sent it to a publisher in Turin who published the Dutch best-selling author—a certain Grunberg—and they accepted it immediately. So, *Het strand van de romantische honden* became entirely that which it always had been: *La spiaggia dei cani romantici*. It appealed to Dutch critics, as well as Italian ones, and was met with very kind reviews—the Ligurian author who lived in solitude on the Northern coast, etc. It was almost summer, I had a presentation in the cult that is the Bonardi bookstore, radio interviews, and I was invited to meet the Italian Literature students at Utrecht before classes ended. All of them asked me if I was the romantic dog, the professors interested in the most minute details. Naturally, I enjoyed myself very much in saying that yes, it was me. Of course, it was me.

In July, I informed the publisher that I would return to Italy for a short while. While there, I presented the Italian version of the book, but I also spent long periods of time in my hometown, and one day, immersed in the brambles of the Vallonello garden, I heard someone calling my name. It was the grocery woman. There was a call from Holland. I thought it was Piet regarding some review—he kept them all. Instead, it was the shrewd and wealthy publisher, via his interpreter. A Dutch TV channel—number one or two, I can't remember—was looking for me everywhere so we could have a chat. It was a great hook. Great, I said, but I was in Italy right now, in the brambles, in the part of the garden where so many years before a poor mole had emerged, and I would return to Holland in September and would be able to meet up then and have all the chats they wanted. The publisher was furious, he yelled at the interpreter, who translated both message and tone as they yelled at me in duet. September was too late, I had to return now. I had things to do now, I said.

There were these Genoese tourists in the grocery store—a husband and wife. Unaware of what was happening, they looked at me worriedly. I put a hand on the receiver and introduced myself: please excuse all this, it's my Dutch publisher, I'm Marino Magliani, the writer. Then, I returned to the call and the continued yelling, threatening they'd challenge the contract.

XXIII

I found a very comfortable scarf in a used clothing store, one of those neck scarves that you don't tie but you insert like a wool collar. I suggested Piet get one.

It keeps you warm and you don't even have to be worried about tying it poorly.

In the last few days, the snow has hardened and has made my walks more perilous. The resident wouldn't take notice of anything unless, while walking across the enormous television that's always on (that is to say, the window), you had shown them a scene in your new neck scarf and two hats as you stumbled to regain your footing, grabbing onto a spiny branch or a lamppost and not knowing how to go on.

Today, the snow is melting, but it is still cold and windy, and everything ices over again at night.

I stomp my feet on the sidewalk, I wait for her to see me.

I haven't written her anything else about sunsets.

There. My heart . . . She smiled at me; she had her paper ready. She presses it to the glass. I cross Ursa Major, the sidewalk on her side of the street, I ask permission to enter her garden, permission granted, I climb over the wall, I move to the window, I bow halfway and I'm a few inches away from her eyes and her neck which is set in her athletic shoulders, the freckles on her face, her small ears like Vermeer's *Girl*. Her breath fogs the window . . . She's looking at my neck scarf, I hope she likes it and that she doesn't find it an insult to her own small neck.

She signals for me to read.

Wat een mooie ondergang, heb je nog meer?

That beautiful *Sunset*, do you still have it?

I take off my gloves, rush to take the tape, scissors, and folded paper from my inside pocket. I hang it.

Her (lips): Wait.

She writes on her paper in Dutch: Nice scarf, sunset boy.

Jonge isn't exactly "child," it's also "boy." This, I note, is certainly a hook.

I nod to her again, backing into the gravel.

She (through lips and gesture) begs that I am careful around the beautiful vase of *Adian Rad Fragrans* laying on the gravel, growing in a cascade like the maidenhair fern in the Sorba fountain. Indeed, in completing these taping missions, I often trample its flowered tentacles and hear them creak under the snow, but I always pretend not to notice.

I stop for a moment on the far sidewalk, I look and see she can't see me because she's reading my dark and smiling.

Then I tell myself to let her read. I raise my neck scarf my chin, the collar, put my gloves back on, and hear my footsteps muffled by snow and dreams. It's raining, light and coming down sideways, illuminated by the orange lamplight. I think of her, of *The Dark* (the original Italian of which I reproduce below), of my Ligurian vegetable gardens, of the drizzle making soup of her *Adian Rad Fragrans*.

I walk aimlessly, my hands in my pockets. Piet is sure that one day we'll be able to make dreams on command, there will be a machine with a program into which you enter some coordinates—wet dreams, for example—and one can sleep well-prepared with a towel on the sheets. It must be beautiful. A second life.

The Dark

There was a darkness in town, Anneke, that resembled the dark in churches, the kind of dark that is sculpted around candelabras and chandeliers, the kind that only exists because somewhere else there is light. It wasn't night, but the darkness of porticoes, the piercing of an arcade. It was the naked geometry of the aisles of San Giovanni del Groppo.

Despite how dark the church was, its high windows burned with many colors. In the summer, those windows, whose stories I could never see, betrayed flying creatures as they passed. (Now I know they were actually the windows' own sacred mysteries.)

And when I'd return home, the dark would greet me with the silence of the stalls. I watched and breathed through the cracks in old doors. In the warmth of tails and failing gestures, the animals tried to shake off flies to no effect. The sound of silent hooves sunk into manure. The constant activity of jawbones was a chatty language. The ox spoke, said he's here (which the ox realized from the strip of light missing from the large crack in the door), what does he want, can't he let me eat in peace, do I bother him while he eats? They would say things like that, and they watched me even when they couldn't see me. A rope held the doors shut. My mother, afraid of hooved animals, didn't allow me to enter the stalls. I could only watch from outside.

The steer was red, a plow and packsaddle awaited him in the walkway. Smoking, humid nostrils, the vice of mastication even when not eating, a tic that I thought I might also have. It drank with a deep-violet tongue. The mule had hard, ashen skin and big yellow teeth. The goat struck the wood with its horns. The rabbits snuck behind the stone and, after a short while, escaped to sniff at the air.

At night in my bed, I would peer through the other crack—the one made by the shutter when it was open about four fingers wide—and look up to the moon, high in the night sky. Tomorrow never existed with the dawn so far off, even if I dreamt of you. The world outside, seen from my own stall. And I laughed, sometimes, if I wasn't moved to tears.

XXIV

What do the residents of Zeewijk do when they are no longer independent, as Piet soon will be?

The place is called *bejaarden huis*. There are at least three of them and, like everything in Zeewijk, they exist in rotation: Now they build the nursing home in one location and, in twenty years, they will in another. Thus, someone who lives in Zeewijk is never able to identify with a specific location, but only with the idea of this home. This vaguely unknown destination fosters something like fear; One walks through the constellations and wonders, Will it be here in the square on Aquarius, or will it be up on Pegasus?

Usually, these homes are very well taken care of, a tiny garden for the elderly to keep up their energy with their little "private" garden, a reward for their career, a window from which they can watch life pass by. The elderly of the *bejaarden huis* are serene. They own their studio apartments and have everything they need: a nurse that comes by to check in on them, a kitchen, a bathroom with support bars, and even a view of cherry blossoms.

I see them in June, on their plastic chairs outside in the Nordic breeze. It seems like they check on the wrinkled green cherries, waiting for them to mature, but they won't ever mature because we're in Holland and the old people know that. Who knows what these old people are thinking?

Maybe, Piet reasoned, it's like that in Liguria—there, in that place where you were born, where there was a hospital and where now the elderly people sit on white seats with some desire but to watch the clusters of dates that will never yield fruit.

I don't know, I told Piet. I don't ever speak to him very willingly or at length about the idea of a home. I'm not the right person, I confess, and talking about beginnings and endings confuses me. I wish to see you if you were born somewhere that now holds a sunset.

XXV

At Christmas, Zeewijk sparkles with color and lights that flicker and vibrate, that rise and fall. A sparkling grey Zeewijk.

For a handful of days, I saw Anneke again through her window.

I thought: That glass there, for he who looks at her, is a lens, the way to see desire—the dates that will never mature—but it's also a window that holds that dream at a distance, like binoculars held the wrong way.

Every so often I reread both *Sunset* and *The Dark* to convince myself that I'm doing a good job. Yes, you're making a good impression, I tell myself. I'm completely convinced. It's a little like those on-demand dreams: The narrative material that I use is the program, my writing the machine. The result is certain. One day soon, the dream will come true, it just depends on the machine, on me. One day soon, she will appear and will pull me inside.

She likes me, Piet, I tell him.

Sometimes, when she's not there because she's at work, I stop and take in the things crowded in her front garden—one of the Seven Dwarves in half-faded ceramic, a cascade of plants, a lantern with no light, the white gravel of the garden, two pines, two *pinus pimilia* of Siberian glauca, also the dwarves and plants bordering the other property.

One time, I surprised her—though it would be more accurate to say that she was the one who surprised me—in front of her house. She arrived from work on her bike in her hooded down jacket and with her reddened face, her tired eyes. She barely smiled at me. I put my hands up as if they were binoculars to see the effect it had to see her in that way. She couldn't help but laugh and walked down the alley to her back garden and the small shed where she stores her bike.

I didn't walk back there, even if it is still accessible to the public. I didn't think she would like that.

The things we write each other these days are very beautiful.

Her: I liked *The Dark* and the animals from your region a lot.

Me: The animals of Zeewijk are fascinating, too. Today I heard blackbirds and a thrush.

Her, some hours later: Where I work there's a glass ceiling and you can hear the rain and the gulls the gulls the gulls.

Me: I hang small nets on the terrace with balls of food that contain more fat for winter, and Great Tits and even crows—with their icy blue eyes—come to eat.

Her: Ha ha their icy blue eyes.

Me: I saw your Christmas tree.

Her: Have you put one up too?

Me: No, but my friend Piet has.

My last message, accompanied with a bow: With the cold in the forest, the foxes are coming closer to look for food.

I passed by again ten minutes later. She was on the telephone, laughing, but she didn't see me, so I let her be.

I passed by again after a half hour. She was reading, seated on the sofa, her feet in a basin of warm water, as all Zeewijk's fish cutters' are when they return home from work. She realized that I was on the other side of Ursa Major, but she didn't get up. She's tired, I told myself, so I just raised my hand and walked away. She's tired.

XXVI

In the last couple years, it's become fashionable to have a bare back garden, often lined in modern bricks different than those of the street—pink-colored cobblestones nested together like fishbones and slight arches, a faded wooden bench bolted and chained so that young punks won't take it away, and nothing else. It's a fashion of a garden in poverty, something minimal. However, there are residents that don't follow what's in fashion and, instead, have opulent gardens full of vines that climb and enlace, some even with a pool of water that swells with snow in the winter or remains black and putrid, full of stagnant life.

In the evening, if there is no snow, I like to walk with my eyes closed. I recognize places based on their scent. Between Fahrenheitstraat and Dolfijnstraat, after passing the smell of one of those pitiful ponds, you can proceed unobstructed, provided your hand is in front of you so you don't hit the lamppost. Following the wall as it gently turns the corner, you arrive between Cepheus and Grote Beer—Ursa Major, the Great Bear.

Now, at this point, if you open your eyes, you note that above a door on Cepheustraat there is a light on. After a few minutes, it will turn off.

It's moving, isn't it, Piet?

It's a favor—a gift—from life. Knowing that a light will turn on as you walk by. At any time of night, without even meaning to, you must exist. You don't have to insist or demonstrate it, you don't have to sound a horn or scream or put on a record. You don't have to write a story in the hopes that the world will stop for you, notice it, read it. You don't even need to lament that you're the only greatly misunderstood man on this earth! You walk on the sidewalk, you pass by, and, if the light turns on, you exist.

Piet lowers his eyelids and he nods.

I'd told him that the other day, while writing *The Dark*—then translated perfectly suitably by him—I returned to Liguria.

The church of San Giovanni del Groppo, the dark and the colorful designs of the window and the stories they told still unsure to my eye. The portico, the empty stalls.

And Vallonello, Gilun, Pozzo, Robavilla.

I went into the brambles again. As Anguilla would say, I don't miss them, but I do think about them.

XXVII

Zeewijk, December 22, Grote Beerstraat 18:00

She doesn't even think about me anymore. I should explain; It's not entirely true to say that she pretends nothing's happened. Now, I pass Ursa Major and my heart beats faster—one window, two, seven, ten, and then hers, the twelfth (or twenty-seventh if I'm coming from Orionweg)—and I stand there for a moment and if she's home she raises her hand but immediately returns to what she was doing before. I can't stay there a moment longer, so I leave. I run past the eleven windows that separate me from my last sidereal crossing or I retrace my steps towards Orionweg if that's the way I came.

These are moments when, without being conscious of it myself, I go out of Zeewijk, pass Orion, traverse Jupiter, careful not to slip on the sheets of ice. The boys who hide under some palazzo to smoke a joint recognize me and squawk at me like seagulls. I shoot back a call like a cold-eyed crow, a single broken cry, leaving them to whatever they're up to as I continue on.

I stop past the houses, on the first set of dunes, in front of the great scroll of the sea.

What had I expected?

Maybe, at the end of it all, what you regret is not being so daring. It's nonsense to think that those who have been might regret it even more.

And what does it matter now . . .? When I'm on the nighttime dunes, I watch the strip of sky above me and breathe in the salt, a deer notices me and escapes into the bushes.

There's nothing in this air, alive or dead, that can transport me to a Ligurian portico.

Fireworks between the houses. A test. Everyone hates these games.

And maybe it's here that these games do effortlessly manage to remind me of Liguria, of a Liguria that's distant and stupid. We had a tradition of pranking even in our part of the world. The game was cruel, it was. Playing tricks on old people to try to get them to run after you. It was like this: At night, you knocked on a door and then rest took off from there. Whoever was hot on the tail of the pranksters would run up a flight of stairs, under a portico, do two quick passes of the *carruggi*—those narrow Ligurian alleyways—would cuss and swear and would chase the dark. He would know who he was chasing and that they'll never be caught. It's a vulgar tradition. Nothing ever happens in this town, the youth say to themselves, pleading their case. But it kills time. And that's its real error: Time should always be saved. Because time dies anyway, even when you don't try to kill it.

In dialect, it was called the game of *scure*, which means "flowing." It probably has another name, or maybe it doesn't have a real name at all, but it's a cruel game that's played everywhere.

In Zeewijk, the world's litmus test, this kind of prank couldn't be missed. It's called *Luilak* and is a tradition that is kept alive in various parts of Holland. On the Saturday night before Pentecost, it's even openly tolerated. It consists of a good bit of noise: boys under 15 wake those who are sleeping, throw eggs against windows, and run away to hide themselves until dawn.

The next morning, I find Piet hard at work, his window brush soapy as it strips away fresh egg whites and a full year of salty spit.

Luilak. We did it too when I was young and lived in Ouje IJmuiden, he tells me, a half-smiling window cleaner.

Maybe the boys know you, target you specifically. Your neighbors' windows have been spared, I tell him.

He laughs harder.

It's strange to speak of tradition in a place that was born in the Sixties.

Besides *Luilak*, the people of Zeewijk maintain the traditions of November 11 and December 5, the latter of which I've already told you about.

The former is Sint Maarten. Children prepare paper lanterns with small candles inside and then, from the 17th to the 18th, they go knocking from house to house, with hope and empty bags. The youngest are accompanied by their mothers, the older ones in small groups of three or four. They knock and sing the song of Sint Maarten.

Elf november is de dag
  dat mijn lichtje
  dat mijn lichtje
  Elf november is de dag
  dat mijn lichtje branden mag

("November 11 is the day when my little light may burn.")

The homeowner opens the door and puts a handful of candy, a mandarin, cookies into each bag.

Little by little, Piet, we lose our traditions.

Piet nods. When he was a boy, hundreds of groups would come by the house. Now, only a few, and we wait for the song that will never arrive.

I buy enough candy for forty children, and only a few half-frozen ones will walk Bellatrix, singing shyly and leaving with their prize.

December 5, however, is Sinterklaas, and Saint Nicholas arrives from Spain with his white beard and gifts for all. Two little men of color travel with him, the mythical personages of *Zwarte Piet* dressed as pages. Every country has invented its own obscure character for the fantasy of children, France's Père Fouettard, Germany's Knecht Ruprecht, Austria's Klaubauf. It's strange how every country has to identify its devil with a person of color.

XXVIII

Anneke didn't go to work. I passed by at 3 in the afternoon and saw her walking around the house with the vacuum, the cord in her hand like a leash. I had written something beautiful. I took off my gloves, felt around in my pocket for the folded paper and the adhesive tape to show her what I'd brought her, but she pretended not to see, smiling at me and giving me a thumbs-up as if to say everything was okay. Yes, of course. Everything's okay.

From afar and with just my lips, I wish her well, and she replies likewise—or at least that's how it seems—before she turns back to walking the vacuum.

Her window gleams. I remember the first time, her first smile, and that piece of paper. When I got home, I couldn't believe it, I kept telling myself that I'd made everything up, so I came back and approached the window like a thief to discover our fingerprints on the window.

Piet jokes about it, pulling out the dumb things he read in Caribbean novels. Why don't you write her a quick note asking if you can water her back garden?

All joking aside, I really would like the chance to explore Anneke's back garden.

In Bellatrixstraat, I don't have a garden; *maisonettes* enjoy only a small terrace on the bedroom level and one on the living room level.

For the residents of Zeewijk, the back garden is a secret place, somewhere I will never be able to enter, rendering my reports into half-seen gestures. I walk around the houses and along the small paths between one property and another. On my sides plank fences from Ikea or Gamma rise along panels and vines, young saplings whose leaves conceal secrets.

The only back garden that I can say to know well is Piet's. Why, I asked him, would you spread your front curtains wide open to show the world what you're cooking, what you're watching, your children, your taste in husband or wife as they sit on the couch, and then hide your back gardens away from the world?

Piet had no explanation.

When it's nice, unlike now, and when the plants aren't rotting in the rain and snow and as Piet prepares dinner, I'll often open the back window of the living room (without letting Piet know, since he already knows what I'm about to do). I go down to his back garden and investigate. Not his rickety flowerbeds, which I know by heart, but instead I study other things intently, leaning a plastic chair against on the creeper-covered fence to discreetly look over into the neighbor's back garden. I look to see if they've moved their plants, any new grafts (his neighbors are very active in that sense). I can even see a part of the next neighbor's garden, so I move the chair to do the same with that garden. As a natural first step, I always make sure not to be seen, but there are times that I am discovered, despite my caution.

Are you looking for something? they ask politely. Are you a relative of Mr. Van Bert's?

No, I respond. I'm his close friend, Marino Magliani, the Italian translator from the Spanish—Carlos Alberto Montaner, Fernando Velázquez Medina, Gabriel Miró, for example. As for the Dutch, I've translated the cult poet Marsman and I'm the same poet and narrator whose Dutch translations are by way of Serena Libri and Prometheus, and who also was the subject of a four-page interview with published in *Vrij Nederland*.

All right, but what are you looking for, they say from their side.

Nothing. I was looking at your garden. I love back gardens.

I know at least ten or so back gardens whose fences allow someone walking by to glimpse a few details. I place my eye between the posts, as I used to do as a child through the cracks in the stall doors, and I can see a bench, a sheet, a swing, a pigeon cage. If I'm lucky, my eye can even capture the owners amputating some plant or sitting and taking in the sun.

You're so different when you're in your back gardens, I noted to Piet. All of you.

He says that I'm exaggerating, but I know it's true. They transform. I see them in their back gardens—on their lawn chairs or propped up on their hoes in thought, absent—and it seems like they're almost one with the earth.

Piet rebutted, And when we're in the living room?

I thought and told him I didn't know, that someone in their living room is present, concentrated on something like a fisherman. A single glance that flits from the television to the window, from the television to the bobber, to what must always be watched.

They're fishermen who never actually pull anything up. I pass their windows, but I think I'm really passing behind them because I don't represent the world that stands before them—no, they are the world, and I'm only someone sliding off their backs and because of this they don't see me, don't recognize me at Mass or in shopping centers or at the gym. And that's why they never tell me that I'm the one who's always passing by.

Bernardo Soares can watch the world because his window above Lisbon has shutters on the inside, too.

But the people you see in there—I'd asked Piet some time ago— the members of their nuclear family, or maybe visitors, everyone in candlelight like the characters in *Casa d'altri* . . . Have you ever realized how strange they are? The way they're positioned, seated on the couch or a chair while they wait for me to pass. They're the most contorted poses I've ever seen in the light of day . . . As if the glass distorts them. If they were on a tram, for example, they wouldn't sit like that . . .

Like what, he asked.

Like they do, Piet, you know like what. You're bad at lying, you know what I mean. They're freakish poses.

Maybe it was time to show me something, he said. And if he hadn't done it sooner, it was only because he was always waiting for me to ask him about it.

It was rare for us to leave Zeewijk—even for just a trip to the sea, a walk in the forest-colony, every time our feet planted firmly in the sand. But this time, the bus took us beyond those borders, we left the coast for Haarlem. We crossed Grote Markt—the market square with the Sint Bavo cathedral in the back, the one where Mozart would play the organ as a boy—and we entered the Frans Hals Museum.

Piet went straight to *The Regents* and *Regentesses of the Old Men's Alms House*.

Among Hals' last works.

The regents look at you, Piet said. They fix their eyes on you and you look at them like a passerby outside the window.

They, the residents of a window, are not a point of view. Every move they make is tied to the time and space of the person outside.

They are the light that turns on as you pass by.

I almost couldn't respond. I thought about what he was saying, about things that depend on other things and things that you say just to say something when you're standing in front of a painting, even if I felt that in all of this there was still some kind of meaning. Then I got distracted—I was thinking about Geerten Meijsing, the Haarlem writer, the author of *Kerstnacht in de Kathedraal*. Meijsing refers to another cathedral, not the one in the market square, but the newer one, the Niewe Sint Bavo at Liedsevaart 146 on the edges of Haarlem. Every time I go to Haarlem, I think of that church and that book, where I went to take notes and which I translated around thirty pages of. A multiple *nostos*: I was returning from Haarlem and thinking of the story of a man who returned to a cathedral after twenty years to search for some graffiti he'd scratched on one of the columns as a boy.

When we left the Frans Hals, we took the little boat bouncing over the canal waters at a high speed, disembarking on the biography of Amsterdam—the Amstel river. Then, a train took us to Den Haag, and we ran to the Mauritiushuis before it closed to look at Rembrandt.

The Anatomy Lesson is enormous.

Piet whispered Sebald's theory to me.

He said: Look at the eyes of the scholars who are presenting the lesson and let's imagine that day. It's winter in 1602, the cadaver is that of a thief—recently-hanged—named Adrian Adriaanzoon. The surgeon is Nicolaes Tulp. According to Sebald, Descartes and Thomas Browne were also present in order to study the steps of the dissection . . . Let's concentrate on the left hand of the cadaver: Tulp's scalpels have cut open the skin and it has been opened to reveal the flesh. The scholars—not all of them—observe the naked tendons of the hand. But does it look like a normal hand to you? It's gigantic—which Sebald makes us aware of. Rembrandt has miscalculated the scale, but also the form, position, everything. The tendons in the hand, the left one—look carefully. They're on top and the thumb is to the left when it should be on the right. Why aren't the surgeons aware of such a deformity? Why did Rembrandt create that perfect mistake?

When you pass in front of a window, you find the strangenesses inside, the unclear and unnatural poses, and you blame them on the speed it takes to bat an eye. So, you return a half-hour later and this time you're sure—you are—that the residents of the window really do cross their legs in impossible ways, that their shoulders are too high and bony, they have mouths you've never seen before . . . So, why?

While he spoke, and while I waited for the answer, the men around the cadaver four centuries ago—almost all with goatees except the cadaver itself, all without hair except the surgeon Tulp—were still (and some looked at me). And I waited for the answer.

He whispered in my ear so the living nearby, also looking at the painting, couldn't hear. They—all those men with the goatees around Tulp—can't possibly be aware of the hand's deformity, just like the residents behind their windows in Zeewijk.

For those who are on the other side of the glass, the capacity to notice their own deformities or those of the people around them is negated—but not to me, I say.

Bingo, you've understood Rembrandt's lesson. He has allowed you to marvel at the anatomical mistake while the eyes of those present at the lesson that wonder are negated, to use your own word. You are Rembrandt, an eye hurriedly passing before the window to capture an eternal glance.

*

On our way back, we stopped in Amsterdam for a few hours. The
waters of the Amstel and its canals flowed calmly, and here and there
I passed bridges the shape of donkey's backs that I'd pedaled across
with Roland Fagel while *Amsterdam is a Butterfly* was being written.
It was a small book, a travelogue for cyclists. I really enjoyed writing
it, lying about my intimate knowledge of the city-world, which, in
reality, is scarce at best. Another publisher, on the back of that small
success, asked me for something else about Amsterdam. They gave me
some money and the Dutch embassy in Italy secured a sponsorship
for a tour through some Italian cities. Excited, I responded that after
Amsterdam is a Butterfly, I would have happily written *Amsterdam is
a Millipede*, in which I'd explain how it's impossible to see the city
from a bike. They never responded.

XXIX

The weather is dry, an indirect light pierces Bellatrixstraat and sets the thirty or so windows of the Schiplaan ablaze. The Schiplaan is the building at the far end of Zeewijk, the one that tourists headed to the beach see in the corner just before reaching the dunes. It used to be that you never saw this show—beautiful giants grew along Bellatrixstraat, the twigs of which formed their own gallery, even in winter. The giants bothered no one, but the City decided to cut them all the same, and, in their place, they planted evergreens that stood only a meter and a half tall. This thing about the trees that were cut infuriated the residents. The City sent a letter to all the houses on the street alerting them that chainsaws would pass that same day, so the residents protested in newspapers, made posters and hung them on their windows: *handen af van onze bomen.* "Hands off our trees." But it didn't matter, that same day the City came, blocked off the road, cut down the trees, threw the branches in a woodchipper, then left and light began to arrive where once there was shadow.

The flora, too, is a part of Zeewijk's eternal becoming.

Grote Beerstraat,
> *December 24*
> *Early afternoon, which means that soon it will be pitch dark.*

She's home, laughing and drinking from a chalice, her red hair a fire over a black sweater and short skirt. She laughs and because of the way that she's sitting—the way that women cross their legs—her miniskirt covers only half her thigh. She has black stockings, adjusts her hair, and while she throws her head back in laughter, the head of a man seated near her turns up, too. And he laughs, too. They're laughing together. He lights a cigarette, protecting the small flame as he would if he were standing outside in the wind. Is this a sailor's habit? Does he work on the docks, too? Or on a fishing boat? Has he returned for the holidays? Is this her boyfriend, her husband, a lover she met while on vacation? Or are they two friends laughing?

What does it matter . . . I keep walking to Orionweg, or I'll likely take a cross street—some minor star, a constellation at the edges of the Great Plain—and I'll walk with that pathetic smile that precedes the only word I know in cases like these. Patience. Maybe I'll go to Piet's, or maybe I won't—he would ask questions, want to know if he's a sailor or maybe a dockworker on the North Sea (where he worked, too, for three months in 1982 when he landed in Stavanger in Norway and met a woman who loved to bend over doggystyle and knew how to say like a doggy in all languages) or maybe a fisherman aboard one of those vessels rusted by sea spray and docked in the port at Christmas, the ones named after mythical fishing cities: Katwijk, Urk, Scheveningen.

What does it matter . . .

It's better that I get back to my book, which is practically finished and only needs to be edited. A few more days, a few more ideas that pass through my head.

XXX

The best time to find Piet Van Bert out on a walk is at dawn.

Piet has no dog, and someone walking the streets of Zeewijk with their hands behind their back—stopping beneath the trees to wonder at how birds build their wind-resistant nests or passing from one sidewalk to another and circling the obstacle—without a leashed dog is no common sight.

You feel out of place when you're on the street alone, when you're bombarded by gulls wherever you stop, at every crossing or beneath the skeleton of a cherry tree. It's not that you're suspicious, but in the eyes of those who are "armed" with their dogs as they pass, you always present a kind of unease. You're not one of them.

The wind pulls at you, surprises you. More than once, you have to grab onto a lamppost and then it seems like against all odds—and I see this—a dog gives you balance. And it rains, not too hard, but an umbrella is unthinkable since the wind would just turn it inside out. It's a man's act of solidarity with his dog. He gets wet, too, since a man with a leash never carries an umbrella—just a hat. Besides, he knows the umbrella wouldn't last long. Consider this: A broken umbrella still peeks out from every trash bin in Zeewijk, and if you pull it out, you'll discover that it has been reduced, literally, to pieces. But this isn't solely the work of the wind: Don't be fooled into thinking the wind is that strong. It's the delusion of a man who has opened it four times in two minutes, the bumbling wind turning it inside out each time, and he has closed it up backwards again and again, after which the umbrella doesn't know what to think, surrenders, and becomes essentially useless—three sprained whalebones, one of which is likely broken and will no longer keep its part of the covering open. The incautious will no longer open it—it's junk—and they'll fold it with their knees out of rage and throw it in the garbage.

When it comes down to it, the dog is an excuse to put on a hat and leave the house. I would like to write a book about the umbrellas and the dogs of Zeewijk and their marginal regency. I've already found the title: *I Am My Dog*.

It's the response that I give to people at night, when I happen in the middle of the people shoved together by the extension that is a leashed dog. I feel naked when I see them talking to one another—each one about their own dog—or speaking to their dogs. Sometimes, those who already know me ask: Excuse me, sir, your dog?

I am my dog, I respond.

Aside from the weather, the Zeewijk sunrise is incredibly beautiful. Simply because of the traffic, which gives the sense of the beginning of the day, not with street traffic, but with air traffic. The Schiphol airport is about thirty kilometers away. The airplanes arriving from Southern Europe, before landing at Schiphol, lower and make a small trip over the North Sea, almost to Zeewijk. At dawn you'll see about ten of them.

I think about this, about the little bow at Bellatrixstraat when I take the Nice-Amsterdam (usually, however, it's an evening flight) and I catch sight of the sea and the mouth of the Noordzeekanaal, like a delta, with the small island of Foort Eiland between the sluices and Zeewijk. Then I start to make my seat-mates smile, loudly declaring: Ladies and gentlemen, behold! The Milky Way! I always request a window seat for this exact reason. I look down, even when we're past Amsterdam, and we've long lost the perfect geometries traced by Zeewijk. In that moment, it's almost as if all my thoughts are backwards—and I mean every thought, every book ever written and read—and quotes from Piet come back into my mind, the only ones he knows in his mangled Italian . . .

There is a fat, aged man who flies over a piazza that could be anywhere in the universe, and meanwhile the stars keep turning, and maybe someone is watching us from their infinite observatory . . .

I would recite this citation to my flight mates, but it isn't kind to introduce yourself to strangers only to abandon them entirely a few moments later, each of them taking their hand luggage and disembarking.

In Schiphol, I wait for the long, articulated bus—the 300, which they also call the Zuidtangent—and, in Haarlem, I take the 75 to Zeewijk.

Once I'm on Bellatrixstraat, I place my suitcase on the sidewalk, listen for a moment, and think that somewhere there's a valley that is both sundial and camera obscura, with cliffs that absorb the sunset.

But the sunrise in Zeewijk really is beautiful, and some summer days I even go out to find it myself. I know all the places Piet goes. First, a parador, a small piazza with three benches—three benches next to each other is a rarity in Zeewijk—that overlook the port and its bank of docks, fishing boats moving in their slow rumbles. Or the one near me, in Bellatrix, where light spits through the nebulous bowels of the clouds and where Piet sits, enchanted before the large building with the slanting windows that ascend every level of the twelve-story dawn. Or the square at Zeewijkpassage, from which you can see the baker opening his shop and, at some point, pull out warm croissants.

XXXI

The dunes are cold in the evenings, but Piet still wanted to lay on the thick, wet grass as we used to do so many years ago.

What did that old man used to say? The one from your country?

He who hasn't been born hasn't lost anything . . . I passed through the Great Bear again.

Piet didn't respond.

She was watching television in the arms of the man from the docks, the sailor or whoever . . . Piet!

Yes?

These days, I've felt like she hasn't wanted to read my writing, or even see me anymore. Every time I've stopped and waited for her smile, she's weakly waved and moved away from the window.

It's cold on the grass, but it's Christmas and it's cold everywhere. Piet looks up.

How much longer until you finish your book, he asked.

It's practically done, I still need to talk about Sundays in Zeewijk, about the fish tanks in people's homes, the forest, the concept of colony, and those Flemish painters of the 1700s that loved those ruins in the Italian countryside. It's a few days of work. I've already written it. Soon, the book will be archaeology.

Then Piet said something that could become real, which I put it in the book.

You don't understand what you've got. Your story with her is over once you finish the book . . . I don't know what it means, but I know that it's true.

I never thought of that, I tell him. I look into the deep, starless darkness, my hands behind my head.

Somewhere I read that Camelopardalis, the Giraffe in the Northern Hemisphere, occupies a dark, forgotten part of the sky and that, to us, it looks like a great emptiness in the celestial plane.

Zeewijk, a world without time, I hear him murmur.

It would be better if we got up, but I don't say anything.

Piet props himself up on his elbows.

Now he'll start to name every nebula, every belt and constellation and planet, satellite, every galaxy, every molecular cloud, every warehouse made of hydrogen and plasma and interstellar dust that can be found in Zeewijk, as he always does when we come to collect the small poison that wet grass provides.

Piet points out everything in the sky, arranged as if the neighborhood had fallen from above. But he never names the star of his street. As if he weren't there. He's not there. I've known this for a while, he's disappeared from Zeewijk. It must be his happiness, his Ceylon, his Herisau . . .

I want to waltz, I tell him. Really, I do. I haven't waltzed for decades. I've only been able to successfully dance with my mother. She was the only person whose feet I didn't step on.

He's silent.

Today, using the kind of voices we use while we lie down, I wrote a piece about an airplane, about seeing Zeewijk while in flight. And that thing Tabucchi said came into my mind, the one you knew by heart.

I turn to look at him because I know that made him smile. When I tell him that, he waits for a moment, adjusts his voice, and starts.

"Meanwhile, he looked at the sky above the colored lamps in the piazza da Alegria, and he felt so small, confused in the universe. There's a fat, aged man dancing with a young girl in a square that could be anywhere in the universe, and the stars continue to turn, and maybe someone is watching us from their infinite observatory."

He takes some sand, makes a fist, and each grain escapes as if through an hourglass.

People are convinced that time is there, he said, but you can't hold it and if you can't hold it, it means that it's not there.

How many times has he repeated that Barbour quote about time? Usually, he ends it by saying that he'd like to go hug Julian Barbour in South Newington before he himself runs out of sand.

Did you ever write him? I ask.

Yes, many years ago, but he never replied.

He never wrote him.

There's still time, he said. One day we have to return to Den Haag, I have to show you the place where modern time was born.

It's been thirty years that he's been saying this.

Time was born with Christian Huygens, the creator of the first accurate clock, the discoverer of the Moon of Saturn, of the Orion Nebula.

He leans back with his hands on the grass, his chest back and his eyes raised skyward, and it's as if his voice is trying to find something like piety.

I'm a numbers guy, he says. A guy who's interested in evens and odds. They called me that at school. A numbers guy. Since they first taught me to count to two, I internalize every number I see, every two-digit number has to be divided by the second one and then the first digit must be subtracted from the result, and if the solution is higher than six, then I'm safe. One day, I left the house and I never returned. I went to find something mathematically sufficient. But what makes something sufficient? He looks up, do the Hunting Dogs have sufficiency? I know every number in Zeewijk—the house numbers, the ones you find on license plates—and all of them divided by the last digit are sufficient; death, life, they're the signs that remain inscribed on my sickened world of digits, division done each time you give in to seeing numbers. I would try to fill pages, but they were nothing, just memories . . . Could they have been something without the word *now*? I rarely go out, I catch colds, home, for me, is the safer side of the trenches. At home there are no numbers, no televisions or newspapers, no numbers. The pain of the numbered streets, the first two digits on license plates (or the second the second two minus the first two, if they're the older kind), minus the second two and, if the result is sufficient, you're saved.

I want to ask him to stop talking. I get up and clean my hands on my jacket. I extend my hand, and he takes it, getting up with great effort. Now he'll probably say that these winter breaks, laying on the grass, are poison to our bones. And he'll probably ask me to clean off the back of his jacket, and he'll probably do the same for me. Our jackets are always drenched, scuffed with stardust, for at least three Zeewijkian seasons. They're recognizable, I imagine, from afar by the people, like our hats.

Some boy tries to light firecrackers again. Barrels arrive from the huge Schiplaan spaceship. In a little bit, a siren will sound, and then everything will fall silent. We pass, a wide berth from the Schiplaan, and, wordlessly, we are careful not to happen on the routes of the Great Bear.

XXXII

Zeewijk, December 26,

I wake up at 8. Outside, it's still the dead of night. Fog. The great grey
of the North stays even at night. How much I miss this when I'm two
months into a trip to Liguria!

I'd like to finish my book sometime today or tomorrow. I've left
a piece of paper on the table as a reminder, *Sunday morning* written
on it. Sunday, between first light until about ten, is the ideal time to
gather information on the "bare property"—that is, the uninhabited
window. Rarely before that time will the Dutch in Zeewijk—and
in all of Holland, I presume—appear in their own living rooms. A
fragment of time out of time, grey and tired. The burglar light serves
no purpose, since you can hardly see it anymore. It's a fairytale for
blonde children: Once upon a time, there was a dark window and
there was a light. The burglars came in when the night was over, and
those burglars stole time . . .

I select a series of streets and windows on the way to Pieterskerk,
the small church on Zuiderkuisstraat, where Mass begins at ten. I have
an embarrassment of choices and two hours of time. I don't stop to
view just any window. This is one of those "raised windows," so named
(by me) because you must walk up three steps in order to reach the
door, and the residents on the other side of the glass can look at you
as if from on high. I only wanted to point this feature out to you.
Let's move on to a series of classic windows, instead.

Window 1: A magazine, a pair of glasses, and a small saucer still
lay on a short table. Television off, plants lining the shelf. I see it as
if on the big screen, even what's in the far background—the window

that looks out to the back garden, which I can make out from here. I don't have to hurry along so as not to be seen. It's Sunday; I can pretend to lace my shoe, my foot on two palms on the wall, and for a few minutes I can take in the gift of a show. A singular concession.

Window 2: I can see a sideboard, varnished white in the modern taste. A bookcase taking up a whole wall. In the front garden, there are flowerbeds in wooden boxes and a small wrought-iron fence, the posts of which are more often stepped over than opened.

Window 3: Furniture the color of wood, all with sharp edges . . . Seeing the tables and the seats made of edges, the tables of thick glass, you already know that children do not live here. Sometimes, instead, there is a bow on the door or the window to signify a recent birth and the writing on the ribbon reads *Hoera het is een jongen.* Congratulations, it's a boy. After a few months, you see a box in the corner, and soon the sidewalks are scribbled with colored chalk and every year you see balloons, garlands, evidence of a birth, and the usual ribbon on the window. *Jantje is jarig.* Already Little Jan has a birthday. (How beautiful it is to know that time has kept hold of at least the names we held in our prehistory. There are things in our language that we would never have thought to create. But here . . . here we have a name that contains the memory of a child when he was still a child, that diminutive *je* that will allow Jan to always be Jantje.) And twenty years later, a sheet hanging from the upstairs window: *Hurray! Jan has graduated.*

These chalcographic Sunday sketches are the miraculous mysteries of these windows. A mystic catalog of images. Look at this one. A house that loves animals and we never noticed, the cats napping on the shelves and the dogs who watch you but don't bark. A bicycle chained to a bench, its wheel bent because Saturday's thief wasn't able to carry it with him, so he kicked the rim crooked. And all those plants with the small blue and red flowers, spongy and hardy, the name of which was revealed to me by the salesperson at *Groen vinger.* And the enormous aquarium, bubbling the water's surface as if it were boiling, its pump a beating heart. Glass beyond the windows filled with brightly colored tropical algae. Or, for those with extreme Gothic tastes, a nursery with a snake and lizards. And finally, the paintings. The fake Vermeers, the *Drinkers* of a false Hals, imitations of the *Italianates*. So many dunes, fishing scenes, nets, bits of light on gulls, and so many fakes in general.

No later than ten, I told myself. At ten, my time is over. Around then, the father, husband, or boyfriend will come down, yawning and shuffling about with his hair in tangles, looking around, lost. Sunday is precious, but I don't take full advantage of it. Before Mass I could have taken photos of the plants and interiors, documented the furniture, choose a sample of windows and understood which furniture is most fashionable. Piet continues to give orders—he always takes it seriously when a publisher asks me for a book. He gets upset and, to tell the truth, I get a little tired of it, but I'm also very happy to play at my own game of regal marginality. I'm lazy, to be clear. Regarding the windows and gardens, for example, Piet went to the library and brought home Piet Oudolf's studies, photographs of L.P. Zocher's work (the architect of Vondel Park), and he even read about the Garden Kingdom of Dessau-Wörlitz in German and wanted me to read and explain to him the concepts in Gianni Biondillo's *Metropolis for Beginners*, along with the landscaping of Franco Arminio and Minervino's *Statale 18*. I tried to indulge him, so I read a little of these and told him that, yes, I will take photos and I'll look into it, draw up charts of the most-loved flowers, distinguish the fakes on the wall from the real.

But something did actually emerge from the paintings: The residents of Zeewijk love the *Italianates*, that group of Flemish painters from the late 1600s who were so taken with our landscape. Herds, Arcadia, Roman ruins. Those paintings by Jan Asselyn, Jan Both, Andries Both, and Willem Romeijn. This was revealed to me by a frame salesman and amateur forger. Naturally, I went to review all the paintings in Piet's house, but I found no trace of Arcadia. To tell the truth, from the time I learned this thing about the *Italianates* and the Bamboccianti—disciples of Pieter van Laer, called the *Bamboccio*—I found courage on Sunday morning. I create a screen with my hands over my eyes and I glance at the paintings, but I resign myself almost immediately: You can't see the paintings well, an indirect light takes the walls as confidant and doesn't let you to distinguish between a Roman wall, a trawler boat, and a heavenly scene of little angels in the clouds.

XXXIII

Zeewijk, December 28, almost evening.

Who knows if the man who might have been a sailor from the fishing boat Urk or Katwijk still lives on Ursa Major? I haven't gone by there again.

Love in the time of writing *A Window to Zeewijk*, Piet says. The miracle of a love written down.

Today I'm at his place, but I asked him to stake out Ursa Major. For dinner, he's prepared some rice with pieces of Surinamese chicken that he's good at making, even if it is always too spicy, and that means I'm to bring the water bottle that sits next to my bed.

He asks where I'm at.

I've written Sunday. I still have to write birthdays, and community news.

Birthdays are felt deeply in Zeewijk, and I assume they are throughout Holland. Here, if it's your sister's birthday they won't only offer her well wishes, but they'll offer them to the entire family tree. Guests will arrive, put down their gifts, and shake the hands of every brother, sister, child, and parent of the celebrant, congratulating each and every one of them.

Congratulations on your sister's birthday.

I think it even extends to in-laws, but I couldn't swear to it. The Dutch party can be recognized by sad, popular music played at maximum volume—songs about ships that don't return and small cafés on the port, about fathers who tell their young sons about the bitterness of life—and, finally, they start counting, drinking some beer at each number. And I should add a long chapter here. The Zeewijk resident accepts everything related to the word "beer" with a smile, a moan of pleasure. Should they meet you at the market with a case of beer in their cart, be sure that they will laugh. The same will happen when they pass nearby on the beach in summer, surprising you that they have a beer in hand. Beer makes them laugh before they even drink. Beer is complicit.

Watching a soccer game on tv or during a barbecue, in the garden during the summer or winter, it doesn't matter where; Out with coworkers on Friday night, after the soccer game is over, beer is the prize. There is even a verb, *biren*, that literally means "to beer" and I've even used it myself. (When using it in my Italian books, editors always cross it out.) I couldn't believe it myself until one time, passing near a young couple, I tried not to overhear their argument. She was trying to convince him not to leave, saying: Stay with me. He said that he'd already told his friends he would go. What are you going to do? she asked. We're beering, he responded.

They leave on their bikes and they beer, and with any luck they forget their bikes somewhere and take another, and in the night's silence all that can be heard is the off-key song of a soccer team and their tires running along the bricked paths. There's always some tiny shard of glass (from a beer bottle) between the stones, which is lucky for *Guru Bike*, the shop that repairs tears in less than 5 minutes. They must be fragments of very old bottles, because it's been illegal to drink beer on the street in Zeewijk, and I presume the entirety of Holland, for many years. The use of hash on one bench is more tolerable than the consumption of alcohol on the next.

In Zeewijk, it's really quite difficult to find two benches next to each other. There were a few pairs—couples—when I arrived, but soon they disappeared, one after the other. Sebaste's magical benches.

I ask Piet why there are elms and pines and oaks and horse chestnuts along the roadways—branches and leaves providing relief from summer—but no benches. Does the administration want to discourage gathering? Are they afraid of benches?

After dinner, Piet and I go out. Kids are shooting off illegal firecrackers. We choose safer constellations, a long trip around the shopping center.

There is a small hill of grass with games for children where six cherry trees grow. In late spring they flower and in summer they fruit, but, as I've already told you, cherries never mature here, instead, they stay green until they shrivel up. You look at them and don't think it to be the climate, but the cherries themselves that can't commit themselves to ripening. It's a small plateau with thin paths like a golf course and, in the summer, people walk their dogs and there's a container with small bags for their business. Were there a bench, people would rest for a moment, some would sit and read in the shade of an "immature" cherry tree, like I would, like we did as kids under palms with their dates forever unripe. For this, whoever seeks a bench must walk down the Herenduinweg, the street to Haarlem, passing the two-way cycling path and the gate. In summer, I often go there, select a trunk, and sit outside.

I call the community of Zeewijk a multiethnic park due to its crowding of trees, all different from each other—firs and pines, cypresses and oaks, chestnuts, elms, birches, and the undergrowth of ivy and raspberries and brambles—which the stars seem to have sown there.

It used to be that you had to pay to enter the *Zuid Kennemerland Park*, but that's no longer the case. At the edge of the forest there are gardens that are the property of the City of IJmuiden. People rent and cultivate them. There's plenty of water, Oxheart or smooth round tomatoes planted and fertilized in the grooves of the sand. Piet and I would like to have a rented garden of about two-hundred square meters, a bit larger than Gilun. No fertilizer, it would be made for us freely in the grassy clearings by dozens of highland cows, the Scottish ones with long, brown coats and those incredible horns. We could stock our vegetable freezers for winter. But, the years pass, and we don't rent anything at all.

The woods is also full of uprooted trees which no one uses, as it's prohibited by the forest rangers. The *oost*, or East, *wind*, the one that would tear apart the roofs in Sorba, uproots and overturns trees as if they're stakes. The woodsmen could cut and sell the wood, but they prefer nature take its course: Good wood rots slowly, populating itself with animals and eventually birthing young shoots.

In the other part of the woods, there is a cemetery where Piet's ancestors rest. He brought me there once, an ancient stone greened with moss and inscribed names, all those ancestors and dates, even the writing was ancient. A flowerbed with white gravel and a chain. The impression of a great family fallen.

The part of the woods that faces the sea is the most often frequented by pedestrians, photographers, and impassioned picnickers in its clearings. The cyclist path crosses the pines and penetrates the dunes, connecting Zeewijk to Zandvoort.

You may have heard of Zandvoort—It's famous for its racing circuits, a noise that deafens Zeewijk often on Sundays.

There are at least three noises in Zeewijk: One is from the Zandvoort track, another is the roaring of planes that pass through the air and shade the dunes like butterfly wings on grass. The third noise is the rumbling of the steelworks, which isn't annoying, but can only be heard with a certain urgency. It's an alarm to which you'll eventually grow accustomed. And speaking of alarms, an actual siren sounds every Monday morning between 11:30 and noon. It feels like you should shut yourself in the house when you hear it, but nobody does because, at that time every sainted Monday, it's like a pendulum attacking the antiphon. Nobody cares about it anymore. Instead, a distinct noise is the one around the theme of birthdays, a ferocious beering with music turned all the way up, or a binomial beering—a soccer game on tv. The Dutch are great fans of soccer, and they're also very good at playing it, so such a small country always qualifies for the World Cup and European Cup every so often. However, they have one bad vice: Before every important soccer event, they appear to be the favorites. That is their problem. It begins a few months before, usually on television, with the slogan *Nederland Kampioen* traveling from mouth to mouth and repeated in newspapers, on lighted signs, in advertisements, and even pronounced by babies. Because of this, they've never won anything, except one European Cup.

There are no other sounds in Zeewijk. But the Gabriel Miró quote, that grand narrator of landscapes that I translated with my friend Riccardo Ferrazzi, rings true: (In Zeewijk) all is quiet except silence.

Regarding the community, I would like to linger for at least a moment longer on the local fauna. The giants in the multiethnic park are those Highland cows. When I came to Zeewijk, there were fewer of them. They are resistant to great levels of cold and, physically, they look like Tibetan yaks. They're touchy and don't like to be seen close-up. They begin to nod their heads and they go somewhere else, letting loose a great amount of excrement.

Then, there are the woodpeckers, the owls, every type of blackbird, all except for the lone sparrow who loves stones while in Zeewijk there's only sand. In place of stones, there are bunkers that run along the entirety of the coast and into the woods, casemates connected to each other by an underground network of passages and reinforced concrete posts with slits for mounting cannons.

Other animals present are rabbits that make round holes in the sand and come out at night. Herds of black ponies that let you come close and pet them and softly headbutt your hip, whereas the horses in the park, all grey and yellow, usually run off like the stupendous deer, timid and free, that watch me from the top of the dune and wait for me to see them before they climb over. Of all these animals, only the foxes sometime leave their colonies and search for food between the houses of Zeewijk.

XXXIV

And then, once all that cold passes, warmth shyly arrives. The first tentative sign of a Dutch spring roughly coincides with Queen's Day, which falls on April 30th, but now that Beatrice has abdicated in favor of William who knows if they'll change the date. On that day, Zeewijk's monarchists put the Dutch flag outside their windows.

It's a national holiday and the women transform in a generous explosion of miniskirts and blouses of every color, music on the streets, and rest stops with games for children. I walk around the city alongside Piet, moved by the hope of these great days. In the evening, thousands of plastic cups lay on the ground, and everyone switches to beer, a pleasure to be enjoyed until deep into the night.

Far off by the pond, even the frogs and toads celebrate and pair off.

With a little luck, April nights are calm, and they shine. After the party, Piet and I lay out on the dunes in that spot where we were the other night.

The most beautiful part of every party is when we talk about how we let every last one get away—I mean the women, at least those that were half-available. Sure, it would have been beautiful to spend Queen's Day rolling around on the sand with one of those beautiful Patagonian women with their white thighs and painted lips, the women who made us dream and made us drink, but in the end, they didn't choose us.

You, Piet, (I kept saying over these past years,) you got so close. He would bite his lips and laugh, looking above us. Even now, his eyes reminded me of someone who had always preferred to take matters into his own hand, so to speak.

This is Zeewijk in spring.

XXXV

I still have a doubt about the book, and I spoke to Piet about it.

What will I do about the map of Zeewijk? Will I write the names of the streets in Dutch or will I translate them?

It would be criminal not to let the reader know that Zwaanstraat is the street of Cygnus—that Northern constellation, the one that makes up one part of the 88 listed by Ptolemy. And that Sadrstraat is the second street down from Orionweg and is one of the clearest streets in Zeewijk because Sadr is Cygnus' second brightest start.

Is it a crime not to translate these things or would it seem forced? What changes if the reader knows that Schiplaan is a combination of suffixes to say that building is named so because it looks like a space*schip*?

Or that keplerus is the square for Kepler 11, the dwarf star that has been shining for ten billion years.

And that Camelopardalistraat is truly just the constellation of the Giraffe, the faintest constellation and the one most easily forgotten from Earth, an invisible writer of sidereal prose, relegated to the sharpshooters of cosmic literature with its of fate of living in its own kingdom on the margins.

Piet doesn't know how to respond. I think it's a sin.

XXXVI

Zeewijk, December 29. 90 meters above sea level.
Twelfth floor of the Orionweg building.

One of the news items I've devoted less to during the draft of this
Window—but which I couldn't entirely ignore—is the sight of the
windows in buildings such as this one or the Schiplaan.

I'm not speaking of remarkably stupendous windows, that's obvious.
Each floor has its own passage, an external hallway overhang called
a *galerij*. On one side, the safety railing; the other, the apartment.
There are two windows next to every door: the smaller shows the
kitchen—almost always open-light—and the other is the bedroom—
always hidden behind a curtain. The number of doors, which is to say
apartments, is about twenty per floor.

Orionweg's kitchens are in bad shape and the apartments are usually
rented to young people, students, the working class, the unemployed,
and the asocial. The apartment block will be demolished in 2015 and
the corporation that manages housing in IJmuiden has reduced the
prices so as to rent the space. No one can modify their apartment
(and no one would, knowing that very soon a great club will arrive to
render the building into the sand at its foundation). I don't know what
they will build there instead. I asked Piet, but he doesn't know either.
Three-family houses or fan-shaped buildings—in any case, they'll be
modern housing units inhabited by those who can pay a medium-high
rent. The fate of the students, workers, unemployed, and other docile
fauna is to pass from one of these buildings to another, destined to
live just before demolition. Buildings without maintenance, almost
completely abandoned, and without even a functioning elevator,

gardens completely uncultivated, and window frames corroded by the North Sea's salty spit.

The most interesting thing there is when I walk the external passage on the top floor of the Orion is the show the dunes provide, almost like the Langa, but dotted with bunkers in between sands and bushes rolling down to the sea. At sunset, your binoculars find surprised rabbits, dozens of them, all jumping and chasing each other before night frees the foxes.

XXXVII

I also realize I have said little to nothing about Piet, and I'm happy for that. I've treated him like he's imagined. I haven't revealed so much as the star of his street, the things in his home, his taste in food—which is that of every Dutchman, *stampot, runderstoofpot, haché*, a stew of boiled potatoes smashed with sliced onion, some vegetables or carrots and potatoes with a bit of sausage, the things that he cooks when he invites me over, and remembrances of his mother, protein-rich foods, good food, the kind of food that makes you last the winter.

He doesn't want that. Sharing his world, his mother, describing her through the photographs crowded on his walls.

Piet is getting older. This I can admit. Soon he will leave his house and go in one of those multielderly places, become accustomed to shrinking himself, the second-to-last matryoshka doll. We start in the womb, we move to the cradle, then we live in a house that seems enormous to us until we move into a house that's completely our own— that has our photos of our memories of the womb and the cradle—and it seems that even more is in our reach, that there are moments when we think we want to have the whole world, and maybe for a moment we really do have it all. Then one day, we leave the homes we've grown used to and we're welcomed to Zeewijk's rest homes, and, to us, the least important thing is the sand on which we'll find it. They'll give us a well-studied studio: a kitchen, a bed with railings so we don't fall out, a sofa in the corner, a bathroom with a walk-in tub and a shower with handles so we don't slip. Every matryoshka hosts our orthonym, and then, separately, the little rest home matryoshka comes and teaches us the basics again—we'd had enough time to forget them—and she gets us used to our new cradle. And if this didn't happen, as my friend Utrecht poet Jan Van Der Haar says, it would be a shame.

Dear Piet, I will not profane the secrets of the books that lie on your creaking wooden floors, the stardust on your furniture and the cosmic scent I inhale when I enter your home, or the yellowed things in your back garden.

But you will forgive me one trespass, one sin. I've never confessed it, it's something I did without your permission because I knew you never would have given it. While you were in bed with the flu one day, you asked me to make some chicken broth from those packets you like and I went down to the kitchen to do so. When I returned, you had fallen asleep. You might have been sweating. I didn't wake you. I left the large, chipped blue bowl you'd bought in Delft on the bedside table and I left, silently shutting the door behind me. Light filled the hallway, reaching even the far end with that room where you keep old computers and some gym equipment from the 70s. I had never entered that room before, you'd never brought me in there, and I only knew about those things I listed from that time I helped you bring up a washing machine and glimpsed them from the hallway.

A chance that, even then, I couldn't let pass. So, I approached on my tiptoes, half-convinced that I'd find the door locked, and instead it opened as I turned the handle. I turned on the light—the one in the hallway wasn't sufficient—and you know what I saw . . . You know. I would never have imagined.

Photographs of Zeewijk and Oud-IJmuiden, the old neighborhood where you were born, hung on the walls—pictures of children and adults from the 30s with clogs on their feet, herring faces, a mule with a cart, the port, houses and their frames and the trees of the past, which are very similar to those of today.

And then that incredible drawing that I spoke of in the introduction of this book.

The superimposition of Liguria and IJmuiden, an anguished precision, very few differences between one map and the other, the two worlds coinciding, Cartesian arches of time and space. I had recently taken up the habit of taking photos on one of those cameras that only cost a few florins, and I took some photos there, too.

The superimposition. But that wasn't what surprised me. Piet, we had been friends for almost thirty years, we had spoken of these things a thousand times, why should it surprise me if one winter's day, tired of reading or watching the rain or listening to my stories, you took paper and pencil and traced those shapes? You'd made others of the Milky Way and the constellations that lay upon it, you recopied images of Ligurian terraces, and you had shown me every design. No, it was something else that made my eyes open wide: It was when I approached and read the date under the images.

Zeewijk, October 20, 1964.

He knew, I said to myself. And I was afraid. I was afraid to turn around to find you in the doorway, furious and in your pajamas, afraid that at any moment you could discover that I'd violated your secret. I left everything as I'd found it, turned off the light, closed the door, and tiptoed away again. I went into your room. You were sleeping in the same position as before. The bowl of broth was no longer steaming.

"You knew," I whispered.

When the narrator of these stories, born July 30, 1960 in an old hospital in Dolcedo, arrived in Zeewijk in 1988 and started talking about a land named Liguria and the valley in the far west of the region, you already knew. You, twenty-four years earlier, had already drawn them together, traced their coordinates, designed their constellations. You'd been expecting me.

XXXVIII

I wonder about one last thing, something I should have wondered about sooner.

Won't someone—I mean one of these inhabitants of Zeewijk, these owners and tenants of lodgings with windows—have noticed? I pass them repeatedly, and it's as if they're at a café. They look and they see, but they don't really do either. If they were really looking, they would have seen me, something would tell them that I'm just the one who passes by and casts my gluttonous glances. And if they saw me then they'd know, day after day they would have enough information to create the Magliani dossier. Instead, that scientific part doesn't exist either.

I tell myself, They make you feel like they know who you are—that Italian who's watching them even before your pupils pass over and theirs remain glued to the window—but it's not true. They've never seen you and they didn't invent you. You've walked past and you didn't expect them be surprised anyway. You didn't want them to stop eating their small nuts to let the others on the couch know: Hey, he's back . . .

And yet—it's rare and something I'd rather overlook entirely because it scares me—if you noticed you-know-who behind the glass—since you pretend not to, but you do, in fact, know who they are—you would know you were recognized in that exact instant. He's someone you can't trick, someone who knows that you walk by and look at his shabby *carex comans* or his ivy or pachysandra, its leaves shiny and plasticked, as if you're undressing his house with your eyes.

It took you a while to figure it out. But now you both know everything. And he's at an advantage: He waits for you, he only needs to concentrate on you, but you still have to locate him among four pairs of pupils. You could be wrong. And he has yet another advantage: He does not always live in the same window. And that tricks you.

As an individual, he is the member of a group of at least twenty or thirty residents who don't necessarily know each other or even share anything between them. These people have no trait in common—except, of course, that they're the ones that know—but they probably won't pass it onto their children because it's something that concerns only you and them. They have different ages, belong to different social classes.

The rest is like a game of hide and seek; He ends the countdown as It with a "Ready or not, here I come" and then he looks for you until he sees you and runs back to home base yelling "Found you!" There are some that find you in a matter of seconds. It's the same with the residents who know. They're It. They look for you and, before giving you enough time to disappear from the image (the following window with half a square meter of young bamboo, *fargesia aurea*, in front of it), It spots you in the moment just past his window, and he tells you: Found you.

You count three or four steps, no more. With the first, you take your first step on his sidewalk, but he hasn't seen you yet. With the second you're almost halfway there, and he has found you. With the third—your torso just barely ahead—you're already in the bamboo window's future, even if your back foot is still in the past. No, three steps, no more. Not four.

Anything can be learned with time. For example, there is an effective and tested technique you can use. Once you're in front of the bamboo window, you move forward without looking back, and you could take a gamble at confusing him—he could think that you're not actually you, that you're someone who looked in his window by chance, that crossed his path by chance, but who doesn't look into other windows. You could confuse him (but you won't), and he'll do the same—he could confuse you by changing his position (and his trick won't work either). This is his weapon. Do not forget that Zeewijk is a network of crossings, like the underground bunkers that run along the coast, and the man at home on Andromedastraat in the afternoon can be found in the evening in his brother-in-law's house on Venustraat watching the game or with his work colleague who lives on

Kleperus. A strange community of people that invite each other, as if every birthday, every soccer game, and every Queen's Day was nothing but a pretext to change windows and to breathe down someone's neck. And this is what puts an old scoundrel like you at unease. You're used to looking in the stalls and the fields of your valley, where you always would know the exact things you'd dream.

NOTES

For a long time, Vincenzo Pardini and I have written to each other regularly, once a week. Once a year, we meet in Piazza San Martino in Lucca. We walk down the Fillungo, inside the city's walls, enter into the churches in its walls, and finally return to San Martino. *A Window* had to be born there, during one of those walks.

For some time, Riccardo Ferrazzi and I have written to each other regularly, and once a year we meet in Liguria by the sea near a small island. I describe the North Sea to him, and it seems to me like an exercise. *A Window* had to be born there, in front of a small island.

Regarding the plants in Dutch gardens, an Italian woman living in Amsterdam named Daniela Tasca gave me very precious information. I thank her.

I thank Mike for an idea. And, naturally, Marco D'Aponte and Gloria Fava who inked Piet Van Bert's drawings.

I thank Pablo d'Ors because in reading and translating his work, he introduced me to Anneke.

The quotations on page 108 and 112 come from the celestial plane and from other of Tabucchi's places in *Sostiene Pereira*. Thank you, Antonio.

And to W.G. Sebald and Luigi Marfè, who introduced me to him.

I'm not sure if it's inelegant to use an epigraph at the end of a manuscript, but the following made sense to me here.

> If I look straight up I can see the Swan and Cassiopeia.
> They are the same stars I saw above the Alps as a boy,
> and later . . .
>
> W.G. SEBALD, *THE EMIGRANTS*

Grote Beerstraat (Ursa Major)
Eenhoornstraat (The Unicorn)
Siriusstraat
Venusstraat
Pleiadenplantsoen
Celsiusstraat
Plutostraat
Mercuriusstraat
Cassiopeia
Jupiterstraat
Fahrenheitstraat
Dolfijnstraat
Uranustraat
Poolsterstraat
Herculestraat
Kleine Beerstraat
Watermanstraat
Andromedastraat
Perseustraat
Pegasusstraat
Komeet
Drie ster
Schiplaan
Zwaanstraat
Adelaarstraat
Lynx
Leo Minor
Camelopardalistraat (Camelopardis)
Epsillon Aurigae
Apustraat
Myria (Musca)
Hydra
The Hunting Dogs
Canopusplein
Keplerus
Zuiderkruisstraat

Zeewijk, November 2013 – February 2014
End.

DRAWINGS

The narrator has received some of Piet Van Bert's pencil drawings, from the artist himself, on pieces of paper that time has discolored. The images that represent the superimposition of geographical forms and celestial field, instead, were extracted from photographs taken by the narrator of drawings hanging in Piet Van Bert's secret room. In both cases, we would like to thank Maestro Marco D'Aponte for having inked the works.

LE DUNE

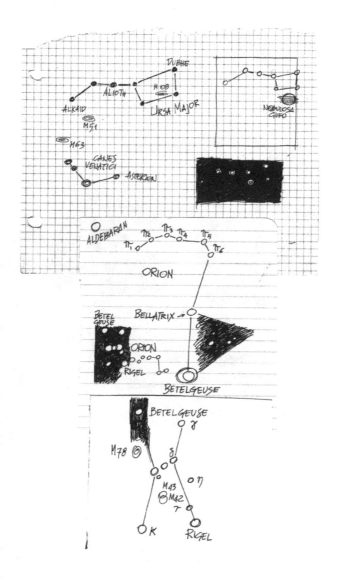

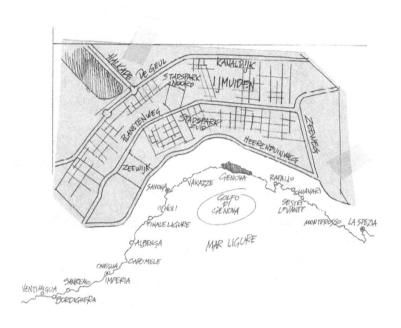

ABOUT THE AUTHOR

MARINO MAGLIANI was born in a small village in Val Prino, Liguria. He lives in Holland, in the neighborhood of Zeewijk on the North Sea. Author of novels and story collections, he is also a translator of Latin American and Spanish authors. Every so often, when he remembers, he returns to Italy.

ABOUT THE TRANSLATOR

ZACHARY SCALZO is a writer and translator currently working in South Florida. He has received degrees in Comparative Literature from Florida Atlantic University and Indiana University Bloomington, and has completed an MFA in Drama from the University of Calgary. His poetry has appeared in *TRANSverse Journal* and his theatrical work has been developed and performed both in the United States and in Canada. This is his first novel-length translation.

CROSSINGS
AN INTERSECTION OF CULTURES

Crossings is dedicated to the publication of Italian—language literature and translations from Italian to English.

Rodolfo Di Biasio. *Wayfarers Four*. Translated by Justin Vitello. 1998. ISBN 1-88419-17-9. Vol 1.

Isabella Morra. *Canzoniere: A Bilingual Edition*. Translated by Irene Musillo Mitchell. 1998. ISBN 1-88419-18-6. Vol 2.

Nevio Spadone. *Lus*. Translated by Teresa Picarazzi. 1999. ISBN 1-88419-22-4. Vol 3.

Flavia Pankiewicz. *American Eclipses*. Translated by Peter Carravetta. Introduction by Joseph Tusiani. 1999. ISBN 1-88419-23-2. Vol 4.

Dacia Maraini. *Stowaway on Board*. Translated by Giovanna Bellesia and Victoria Offredi Poletto. 2000. ISBN 1-88419-24-0. Vol 5.

Walter Valeri, editor. *Franca Rame: Woman on Stage*. 2000. ISBN 1-88419-25-9. Vol 6.

Carmine Biagio Iannace. *The Discovery of America*. Translated by William Boelhower. 2000. ISBN 1-88419-26-7. Vol 7.

Romeo Musa da Calice. *Luna sul salice*. Translated by Adelia V. Williams. 2000. ISBN 1-88419-39-9. Vol 8.

Marco Paolini & Gabriele Vacis. *The Story of Vajont*. Translated by Thomas Simpson. 2000. ISBN 1-88419-41-0. Vol 9.

Silvio Ramat. *Sharing A Trip: Selected Poems*. Translated by Emanuel di Pasquale. 2001. ISBN 1-88419-43-7. Vol 10.

Raffaello Baldini. *Page Proof*. Edited by Daniele Benati. Translated by Adria Bernardi. 2001. ISBN 1-88419-47-X. Vol 11.

Maura Del Serra. *Infinite Present*. Translated by Emanuel di Pasquale and Michael Palma. 2002. ISBN 1-88419-52-6. Vol 12.

Dino Campana. *Canti Orfici*. Translated and Notes by Luigi Bonaffini. 2003. ISBN 1-88419-56-9. Vol 13.

Roberto Bertoldo. *The Calvary of the Cranes*. Translated by Emanuel di Pasquale. 2003. ISBN 1-88419-59-3. Vol 14.

Paolo Ruffilli. *Like It or Not*. Translated by Ruth Feldman and James Laughlin. 2007. ISBN 1-88419-75-5. Vol 15.

Giuseppe Bonaviri. *Saracen Tales*. Translated Barbara De Marco.
2006. ISBN 1-88419-76-3. Vol 16.

Leonilde Frieri Ruberto. *Such Is Life*. Translated Laura Ruberto.
Introduction by Ilaria Serra. 2010. ISBN 978-1-59954-004-7.
Vol 17.

Gina Lagorio. *Tosca the Cat Lady*. Translated by Martha King.
2009. ISBN 978-1-59954-002-3. Vol 18.

Marco Martinelli. *Rumore di acque*. Translated and edited by Thomas
Simpson. 2014. ISBN 978-1-59954-066-5. Vol 19.

Emanuele Pettener. *A Season in Florida*. Translated by Thomas De Angelis.
2014. ISBN 978-1-59954-052-2. Vol 20.

Angelo Spina. *Il cucchiaio trafugato*.
2017. ISBN 978-1-59954-112-9. Vol 21.

Michela Zanarella. *Meditations in the Feminine*. Translated by Leanne
Hoppe. 2017. ISBN 978-1-59954-110-5. Vol 22.

Francesco "Kento" Carlo. *Resistenza Rap*. Translated by Emma Gainsforth
and Siân Gibby. 2017. ISBN 978-1-59954-112-9. Vol 23.

Kossi Komla-Ebri. *EMBAR-RACE-MENTS*. Translated by Marie Orton.
2019. ISBN 978-1-59954-124-2. Vol 24.

Angelo Spina. *Immagina la prossima mossa*.
2019. ISBN 978-1-59954-153-2. Vol 25.

Luigi Lo Cascio. *Othello*. Translated by Gloria Pastorino.
2020. ISBN 978-1-59954-158-7. Vol 26.

Sante Candeloro. *Puzzle*. Translated by Fred L. Gardaphe.
2020. ISBN 978-1-59954-165-5. Vol 27.

Amerigo Ruggiero. *Italians in America*. Translated by Mark Pietralunga.
2020. ISBN 978-1-59954-169-3. Vol 28.

Giuseppe Prezzolini. *The Transplants*. Translated by Fabio Girelli Carasi.
2021. ISBN 978-1-59954-137-2. Vol 29.

CPSIA information can be obtained
at www.ICGtesting.com
Printed in the USA
JSHW031650101222
34643JS00003B/163